YOUNG DOCTORS

Shocked, Brian Denham stared down at the pale face of the unconcious boy in the Casualty Ward ... was his own s... accident, they ... possible? Tob... at the time it ... birthday, and ... from New Zea...

'I'm so sorry about this, Doctor. We've never met your family. If we had . . .'

He had come straight to the hospital from the airport. He had tried to telephone the house a number of times, but there had been no reply – and that had been strange, he had thought at the time, because it was still too early in the morning for Laura to have gone anywhere. Then, finally, as he kept trying the number, she had answered. She had told him in a voice that sounded rather strained that she hadn't heard the phone ringing earlier; she had taken sleeping pills the night before; she had slept very soundly and heard nothing . . .

Also by Carl Ruhen and available in Star Books

SONS AND DAUGHTERS 1
SONS AND DAUGHTERS 2
SONS AND DAUGHTERS 3
SONS AND DAUGHTERS 4
SONS AND DAUGHTERS 5
SONS AND DAUGHTERS 6
SONS AND DAUGHTERS 7

NEIGHBOURS 1
NEIGHBOURS 2

YOUNG DOCTORS

Carl Ruhen

Based on the scripts of
Reg Watson, Michael Laurence,
Tony Morphett, Ron McLean,
Tom McLennan, Ian Coughlan

A STAR BOOK
Published by the Paperback Division of
W H Allen & Co Plc

A Star Book
Published in 1988
by the Paperback Division of
W H Allen & Co Plc
44 Hill Street
London W1X 8LB

Printed and bound in Great Britain by
Anchor Brendon Ltd, Tiptree, Essex

ISBN 0 352 32171 7

1

'Well, there it is. I just wanted to welcome you to the Albert Memorial, and assure you that although you'll be working incredibly long hours here, you'll have the privilege of working alongside some of the finest specialists in the country – and I know you'll learn a great deal from them . . .'

So there it was – the first day at the Albert Memorial, one of the city's major hospitals, on the threshold of a career which, for some of these young doctors, might be illustrious and crowned with honours, united at the moment by a sense of purpose as they listened to the calm, measured voice of the Medical Superintendent as he welcomed them in no doubt much the same words as countless batches of new interns had been welcomed since the hospital's establishment in 1889.

Craig Rothwell stared at the man who was addressing him and his four fellow interns, and wondered at the strangeness of the situation in which he now found himself. Here he was, sunk in an attentive and respectful attitude, listening to the man whose wife, a little more than two hours earlier, had kissed him before hurriedly letting herself out of the motel room in which they had spent the night. 'Thanks, Craig,' she had whispered. 'You've made me feel I'm a woman again.' It had been a wonderful night. She had wanted to be home before little Toby woke up. Today was his ninth birthday.

It had all happened so spontaneously, one thing just leading to another. He had just intended to take her out to dinner then bring her home afterwards – nothing more than that. She had been bored, and lonely, and with Brian not due back from his New Zealand conference until the morning when one of his first duties was to welcome the new batch of doctors to the hospital, it had seemed the most natural thing in the world to invite her out to dinner. All she had to do was arrange a baby sitter for Toby.

He had known the Denhams in Melbourne – and when he learnt that Brian was the Medical Superintendent of the very hospital he was about to join, Craig had telephoned the house. Laura had been delighted. Of course, he must come over straightaway; there was so much to talk about. One thing leading to another, quite effortlessly, inevitably. Laura had told him how bored and lonely she was.

'Since we moved here Brian has been almost fanatical about that hospital of his. It's his life,' she has said sadly. 'If it were another woman, I know I could compete. But not with that vast building – no. That's one thing I can't compete with.'

That vast building in one room of which the new doctors were now listening to some introductory words from the man whose wife had felt so crushed by the weight of the forces ranged against her, and who, during one night in a motel room not so very far away, had been reassured that she was still a woman who could be desired.

There was a knock on the office door which then opened to admit a smartly groomed middle-aged woman Craig recognised as being Brian Denham's secretary. 'You've all met Mrs Gordon,' Brian told his listeners. 'In the short time I've been here, I've found, as you will find, she's one of the few people who keep the place running smoothly – while we take the credit.'

Mrs Gordon smiled at the row of people seated in front of the Medical Superintendent's desk. 'And I also have the nasty habit of breaking up important meetings such as this one, I'm afraid,' she said, then, her smile fading, turned back to Denham. 'There's a problem with the young accident victim. Doctor Shaw wants to operate immediately, but we have no identification for the boy. He'll need your permission to operate.'

Denham nodded. 'I'll go down and have a look at him.' He smiled apologetically at the group of new arrivals. 'If you'll excuse me,' he said as he moved to the door and as the others rose to their feet. 'Mrs Gordon will direct you to the various units to which you've been assigned during this orientation period.'

Shocked, Brian Denham stared down at the pale face of the unconscious boy in the Casualty ward. He couldn't believe it. It was his own son. It was Toby. A hit and run accident, they had said. How was it possible? Toby should have been still in bed at the time it happened. It was his ninth birthday, and Brian had brought back a gift from New Zealand.

'I'm so sorry about this, Doctor. We've never met your family. If we had . . .'

He had come straight to the hospital from the airport. He had tried to telephone the house a number of times, but there had been no reply – and that had been strange, he had thought at the time, because it was still too early in the morning for Laura to have gone anywhere. Then, finally, as he had kept trying the number, she had answered. She had told him in a voice that sounded rather strained that she hadn't heard the phone ringing earlier; she had taken sleeping pills the night before; she has slept very soundly and heard nothing.

'I really called to wish Toby a happy birthday,' he had said.

'Birthday? Oh yes, of course. I'll go and get him. He must be still asleep.'

He had waited for a few moments, wondering why Laura had found it necessary to take sleeping pills, and then she was back on the line, sounding a little breathless, her voice somewhat higher than usual. 'I'm sorry, darling. He must have gone out to play with the kids next door. I'll get him to call you as soon as he comes in for breakfast.'

But he hadn't called – and now here he was, lying unconscious in one of the Casualty ward cubicles. Brian had been discussing a few matters with Raymond Shaw in his office when Helen

Gordon had interrupted them to tell Shaw that a child had just been brought in, the victim of a hit-and-run accident, and that he was required urgently down in Casualty. There had been no reason for Brian to give it any more thought; he has still been trying to reach Laura at home. 'How bad is it?' He tried to keep his voice even.

'He has significant internal bleeding,' Shaw replied quietly. 'Several broken ribs on the left, and these may have ruptured his spleen.' Shaw was looking very solemn. Sister Scott was standing on the other side of the bed. 'If you want to call in another surgeon, I'll understand.'

'No.' Brian shook his head. 'I'd be grateful if you'd do the operation.' He continued to stare down at the inert form of his only son. Today should have been a happy day for him. A party, other kids . . . 'I'll talk to the police.' He looked up at Sister Scott. 'But if you want me . . .'

'Very well, Doctor,' Sister Scott said softly.

With another uncomprehending shake of his head, Brian turned away from the bed. He would need to call Laura who would be utterly frantic by now, and get her over here. The police would need to speak to him, and one of the questions he would be asked was what the boy was doing out on the streets at that time of the morning – and that was something he just didn't know.

'Craig, I've *got* to tell him. I can't see there's anything else I *can* tell him.' Laura was desperate. She didn't know what to do.

She could only blame herself for what had happened. It was no use blaming that silly girl, Carlene, who had assured her she could sit with Toby for the rest of the night when Laura had called her from the restaurant. No problem, she had said. But she hadn't been there when Laura arrived back at the house that morning. Nor had Toby. His bed hadn't even been slept in.

Already beginning to panic, she had called Carlene who had told her that she had stayed with Toby, watching TV, until about midnight, then her boyfriend had telephoned. He had wanted her to go with him to a party, and she had thought it would be all right. She had left Toby still watching TV, because rather than go to bed, he had wanted to wait up for his mother. Laura had screamed at her.

'Laura, for your own sake,' Craig said seriously, 'you mustn't tell him.'

She had called him, arranged to meet him outside the hospital. Toby was still in the operating room. Brian has tried to reassure her that it would be all right, Doctor Shaw was doing a magnificent job – and she knew he had been trying hard to convince himself of this as well.

'I've got to tell him,' she said to Craig as they faced each other in the hospital car park. 'He had to know about us sooner or later.'

'What do you mean? Know about us?'

'I thought . . . when I left Melbourne, I would be able to forget you. Then, when you turned up yesterday . . .'

'Hey, now, hold it right there.' Craig's face was set. 'That little carry-on in Melbourne didn't mean a thing to either of us. It was just one of those things.' Laura stared at him. That was not how she had seen it at the time. Those times when they had been together, and she had given herself to him . . . 'Yesterday, when I called you . . .' he shrugged . . . 'well, I was at a loose end, that's all. I didn't know a soul here. I called you . . . Brian was in New Zealand, and I thought we'd have a night out, for old time's sake. I felt sorry for you, Laura – that's all there was to it.'

That was all? Laura couldn't believe what she was hearing. After what had happened? After that awful risk she had taken, and the mess that had resulted from it? 'You were . . . *sorry* for me?' she whispered.

He took her hands in his own. He spoke earnestly. 'Look, we can go on having fun, if that's what you want – but the situation's different now. Brian's my boss. If you tell him about us, then I'm finished here. We'll both be finished.' He looked steadily into her eyes. 'I'll deny it, love,' he said flatly. 'I'll deny everything.'

As he released her hands, she turned away from him, the tears brimming in her eyes, utterly defeated.

They had saved the woman, they had done everything they could to revive her – and her first reaction had been, as soon as she had regained consciousness, was to blame them for not having let her die. She had wanted to die; she had taken a handful of sleeping pills and washed them down with gin. Hers was the first life Gail Henderson, on her first day at Albert Memorial had helped to save.

Now, still exhausted, still very pale, she seemed a little better when Gail visited her in the Women's ward. 'I'm sorry for all the trouble I caused you,' she said in a faint voice.

'Nonsense, Mrs Curtis,' Gail said with a smile as Sister Scott, a model of brisk efficiency, strode into the room.

'Your husband is here again, Mrs Curtis,' she announced. 'You'll have to have a word with him.'

The woman shook her head. 'I told you, Sister. I don't want to see him.' Gail recalled the fear that had been in her eyes when she had first told Mrs Curtis, shortly after she had regained consciousness, that her husband was waiting to see her. No, she had pleaded then, don't let him near her, she didn't want to see him. She had sounded desperate.

Sister Scott regarded her sternly. She was a woman, clearly, who brooked no nonsense. 'Mrs Curtis,' she said crisply, 'we've more to do here than keep telling your husband you don't want to see him.' With a faint rustle of her well-starched uniform, she turned away. 'I'll bring him in now, and you can tell him yourself.'

Mrs Curtis stared helplessly after her as she left the room, then with an anguished groan, tightly grasped Gail's wrist. 'Doctor . . . please . . . stay with me,' she implored, and Gail could see the fear in her eyes again. 'None of you understand what he's like.'

She was still clutching Gail's wrist as Sister Scott returned with the woman's husband who was looking very concerned. Reaching the bed, he tried to kiss her, but she turned her head away. Her hold on Gail's wrist became even tighter. Straightening, Curtis gave Gail and Sister Scott a quick, embarrassed smile. He looked back down at his wife who had her face still averted. 'Edna, love, there are still some things we have to discuss,' he said quietly.

Tears squeezed out from between Edna Curtis's closed eyelids. 'Go away, Frank,' she said brokenly. 'I don't want to see you.'

'Edna . . .' Curtis glanced up at Gail and Sister Scott. 'If you could just leave us alone for a moment . . .'

'*No!*' Edna Curtis was shaking her head violently from side to side. The tears glistened on her cheeks. 'If you don't go away, Frank, I'll *tell* them . . .'

'Edna, now come on . . .'

'No, Frank!' It was almost a scream.

Sister Scott stepped forward. 'I think you'd better leave now, Mister Curtis,' she said tightly.

Curtis glared at her. Gail saw the hardness in his eyes. She had already decided she didn't like him. She sensed violence only just barely contained. 'But you said I could talk to her.'

Sister Scott's expression was forbidding. 'And now I'm saying you can't,' she returned. 'You're only upsetting her, and that's one thing we can't have.' She indicated the door with a curt nod of her head. 'When she wishes to see you, we'll let you know.'

His eyes narrowed, full of hostility, he stared at her for a long moment. Sister Scott stared unflinchingly back at him. Then, finally, Curtis turned back to his wife who was still tightly clutching Gail Henderson's wrist. 'I'll be waiting for you outside,' he said, and there was no mistaking the threat in his voice. Yes, Gail thought as she watched him walk out of the room, there was violence in the man.

Raymond Shaw had asked Craig Rothwell to join him in the room where young Toby Denham had been placed after his operation. He had shown Craig the scar that was the legacy of that operation. It was a good scar, he had said. What did Craig think? Craig thought he had done an excellent job. Then, when the boy had began to stir, had moaned softly, Shaw had asked him to call Doctor Denham. Young Toby was coming round at long last.

The boy was showing more signs of life. Gently, bending over him, Shaw was encouraging him. 'Come on, old son,' he urged. 'Wake up. Come on now.' The boy moaned again. Returning to the side of the bed, Craig stared down at the boy's face. It was a huge relief that the operation had been a success, but that wasn't enough to banish the guilt he was feeling.

Then Brian and Laura Denham were hurrying into the room. Shaw was still bending over the boy. 'Your Dad's here now,' he said. 'And your Mum. Come on now. Open your eyes.'

Laura Denham's eyes were shining as she stared at the boy from the foot of the bed, Brian Denham had moved to the side of the bed. 'Toby.' He laid his hand on the boy's shoulder. 'Wake up, son.' The boy opened his eyes, blinked rapidly a few times. 'Hello, Toby,' Denham said with a smile. 'Mum's here, too. We're both here.'

Laura moved to her husband's side. Watching her, Craig noticed the slight quivering of her lower lip. 'Hello, darling,' she said.

Toby was staring up at his mother. There was hurt in his eyes, reproach. 'Why didn't you come home, Mum?' he queried listlessly. 'You weren't there, and I went out to look for you.'

She had known that something like this would happen. She had been caught out in one lie – and there were even greater lies to be discovered. She had told Brian that she had been home all night and hadn't heard the telephone when he had tried to reach her because she had taken a sleeping pill. But there had been the question of why the boy had been out of the house at a very early hour of the morning – and the only one who could answer that question was Toby himself. And he *had* answered it. He had been looking for his mother who hadn't been in the house at all. Laura had made up her mind. She was leaving. She had already packed a suitcase and made a reservation at a hotel not far from the hospital where she would stay until Toby was well enough to return with her to Melbourne. They would be much better off back in Melbourne. There would be no more of those fearsome rows, no more tension – no more loneliness in a strange city for which she had no liking at all.

She was just about to call a taxi to take her to the hotel when she heard the front door open, the Brian's footsteps in the hall where she had left her suitcase. She turned to face him as he came into the living room. 'Are you leaving?' he asked.

She had left the hospital abruptly, without a word, when Toby had looked up at her so reproachfully and asked why she hadn't come home. There was no answer she could give him. She had been driven by her shame, her guilt. She had taken a taxi from the rank by the hospital entrance. 'Yes, I'm leaving,' she replied.

'Without a word of explanation?'

'I don't want to talk about it, Brian.'

They faced each other across the room which Laura had taken such great pains to furnish when they first moved into the house. 'This may surprise you, Laura,' Brian said, 'but I haven't the faintest idea what this "it" is supposed to be. All I know is that our son thinks you didn't come home last night.'

She could tell him everything now. She could come right out with it, and tell him the truth. It wouldn't matter. 'I didn't.'

Brian showed his surprise. 'You didn't?'

About Craig Rothwell, and the motel room. Yes, and about these times in Melbourne. 'Yes,' she said simply.

'And left that child here alone?'

Laura sighed. Never would she have even considered doing that. 'I left him with a baby sitter. She said she would stay all night, but she let me down. She left about midnight. Something about a boyfriend, and a party.' What was the use? It was all over now. Enough was enough. 'Brian, don't you think I feel rotten enough as it is without the two of us having another of our blazing rows?' No more blazing rows. She just wanted to leave, go to some place quiet where she could lick her wounds and plan for a future that didn't include him. Craig had told her he had felt sorry for her, had been at a loose end. And then, Toby . . . She was bleeding all over.

'Toby was almost killed, Laura,' Brian quietly reminded her. His face was expressionless. 'Now, I want to know what the hell you were doing last night.'

'I've already told you. I went out.'

'Who with?'

Now was the moment to tell him. It would be so simple just to say that she had gone out with Craig Rothwell, had dinner in quite a nice restaurant, and then made love in a motel room for most of the night. Then she remembered what Craig had told her. He would deny everything. Not that that really mattered; Brian could believe what he liked; it would just be a relief to tell him the truth at last.

'I went by myself,' she said. 'I was in a hotel and had quite a number of drinks. In fact, I became rather drunk. Rather then come home, I thought it would be better to spend the rest of the night in one of the rooms.'

'I don't believe you.'

'I don't care what you believe, Brian.'

'Okay.' Brian spread his hands in a gesture that implied he would just have to go along with whatever she told him for the want of anything better. 'So you went out by yourself, and stayed out all night. Why then?'

'You know why,' Laura replied. They had gone over all this before. 'Because I'm fed up and lonely being in this place day and night.'

'And whose fault is that?' Brian countered. 'You've been invited to meet other doctors' wives. You've been asked to sit on committees . . .'

'I don't *like* doctors' wives,' Laura snapped. 'I don't *like* committees.'

'Then what the hell *do* you like?' Brian was raising his voice; he was losing his temper.

'I like Melbourne. I want to go back there.'

Brian took a deep breath. 'You haven't given this place a chance, Laura. From the very first day you made your mind up that you wouldn't like it – and by God you made sure you wouldn't. You haven't tried to make one friend since we came here.'

'The only friends I want are in Melbourne,' Laura said stubbornly. Old ground, over and over again, the same arguments.

'Friends?' Brian snorted. 'You call them *friends*?' Brian had never liked her friends.

'Yes, I call them friends,' she said coldly. 'They stopped me walking out on you every time you became so obsessed with your precious work that you forgot your wife and son existed. And they even talked me into coming here with you. They thought it might make our marriage work.' Her friends, the ones Brian so despised, had always had the quality of optimism. Once, Laura had shared it with them.

'I see,' Brian said slowly. 'And where are you going?'

'A hotel,' she told him. 'I'll stay there until Toby's well enough to travel. Then I'll take him back to Melbourne.'

'We'll talk about that when he *is* well enough.' He regarded her steadily. 'I think we should also leave the future of our marriage until then.'

Turning away from, Laura let her eyes drift around the room she would be seeing for the last time. She would have to make arrangements for the furniture to be shipped to Melbourne. Perhaps it would be easier to sell it, along with everything else, and start afresh. 'Don't let's kid ourselves about this, Brian,' she said distantly. 'Our marriage is over. After what I did the other night . . .' she checked herself . . . 'after what happened . . .' Her voice caught as, once again, she saw Toby lying unconscious in that hospital bed, so small and helpless. 'I just feel so ashamed.'

She could no longer hold back her tears. She had

been holding them back for so long. She began to sob uncontrollably. Then, numbly, she was aware of Brian's arm around her, his voice as he said, quietly. 'There's no need for you to move out of here, Laura. I'll stay at the hospital.' He gave her a gentle shake. 'Now come on. I'll drive you back there.'

Laura looked up at him through her tears. Yes . . . She had to go back to the hospital. That was where Toby was. Afterwards, when he was better . . . She nodded, then, as he released her and moved back across the room, followed him out into the hall.

2

Edna Curtis was terrified. Frank had come back, and this time there was no one to help her.

They had given her a pill to make sure she had a good night's sleep, but it was slow to take effect; there was too much on her mind; she was frightened; she knew Frank would come back; he wouldn't give up so easily.

After making sure she had taken the pill, the nurse had wished her goodnight, had drawn the curtain around the bed, shutting Edna off from the rest of the ward. A night light glowed softly above her head.

The thoughts crowded in on her. She was tense; she just couldn't relax. At times it seemed as if she were drifting, and then, suddenly, she would be alert again, listening to the sounds in the ward, the muted footsteps and the murmur of voices as the nurses made their final rounds for the night. Then there was silence – and Edna began to drift again . . .

Then, abruptly, she was wide awake, all her senses straining. Somebody had slipped in around the curtain and was standing beside her bed. Somebody in a doctor's gown was bending over her. A doctor . . . No, she realised with a terrified gasp as she stared up at the face that loomed above her. It was Frank, holding a finger to his lips. She opened her mouth to scream. His hand came down across her throat.

'Don't start yelling again, Edna,' he whispered hoarsely. She could smell his breath; he'd been drinking. 'Because if you do, I'll kill you.' She knew he wasn't bluffing; Frank was a man who was capable of anything to get his own way. 'I need some money.'

She had thought, by taking those pills, it would be all over, the constant hounding, the violence. But they had saved her, and he was still hounding her. He wanted money. It was the only reason he had married her, and since she had sold the farm, her farm . . . She shook her head. 'No.'

His hand was still on her throat. He could kill her very easily; he was a strong man. 'Just sign a cheque. That's all you've got to do. Then I'll leave you alone.'

And that was all she wanted. 'You've said that before, Frank.' Many times before. But he had always come back.

'This time I mean it.' Lifting his hand from her throat, he straightened, then reaching into his trouser pocket, produced what Edna recognised in the dim light as her chequebook. He held it out to her. 'Just sign one of them, and then I'll go.'

She struggled up into a sitting position. Perhaps he *really* meant it this time. If she signed the cheque, and if he did go away, for good this time . . . She felt too weak; she couldn't fight him any longer. She looked at the chequebook, then at the pen he was holding out to her in his other hand. She reached for the pen, then the chequebook.

She had just signed the blank cheque and was about to hand it back to him when suddenly she heard voices beyond the curtain, the sound of a trolley being wheeled into the ward. A new patient was arriving by the sound of it. 'Give me a call if she doesn't respond.' She recognised Doctor Howard's voice.

'I will, Doctor.' Sister Scott's voice was very close. Her footsteps came even closer. Frank stood very still above Edna's bed, then, as the footsteps stopped just outside the curtain, he ducked then disappeared under the bed in one swift, silent movement – a split second before the curtain was drawn aside.

'Come now, Mrs Curtis. You should be trying to get some sleep.'

Still holding the chequebook and pen, her heart beating wildly, conscious of Frank's presence beneath the bed, Edna stared up at Sister Scott who didn't look at all pleased by the fact that she was still awake. 'I was . . . I was trying . . .'

Frowning in disapproval, Sister Scott took the chequebook and pen from Edna's unresisting fingers. 'I'll put these in a safe place for you,' she said, slipping them into the pocket of her uniform.

Edna's hand fluttered in the air. Frank was under the bed, and now Sister Scott was taking away the chequebook and blank cheque she had just signed. She was very frightened about what

Frank might do now. 'Please, Sister . . . leave the book. I must have it.'

But Sister Scott was firm. 'You can have it back in the morning, when you're feeling better.' She lifted Edna's wrist and checked her pulse. It must have been racing. She looked at Edna closely. 'Did you take the pill the nurse brought you?'

Frank was only inches away, lying motionless beneath the bed. Edna nodded. 'Sister, I . . .'

'Look, Mrs Curtis,' Sister Scott said briskly. 'You're not helping yourself by getting worked up into a state like this.' Letting go Edna's wrist, she bent over to tuck the blankets more tightly around her. She straightened. 'I'll give you three minutes. If you're not relaxed by then, I'm calling the doctor in to look at you.' She switched off the light. 'Now try to sleep.'

Edna slumped back against the pillows. If only she hadn't come when she had. Frank would have had his cheque, and Edna would have been left in peace – for the time being at least. And now . . . It was the most ghastly mess.

Sister Scott hadn't drawn the curtain behind her when she had gone. Edna stared up at the ceiling and waited for Frank to materialise from beneath the bed. Sister Scott had told her to relax. If she only knew . . .

Then, just as silently as he had disappeared, Frank was coming out from beneath the bed. Hearing the faint rustling sound beneath her, Edna turned her head to watch him as he brought himself up onto his feet beside the bed. His shadow, thrown by the light at the far end of the room spread upwards from the floor as he straightened. Suddenly, from one of the other beds in the ward, there was a scream.

'Nurse! Sister! Quick!' A woman was sitting up in the bed opposite. She screamed again. Frank Curtis didn't wait. With a quick but menacing glance at his wife, he darted around the foot of her bed and ran out of the room. A few moments later, with the woman in the opposite bed still crying out in panic, Sister Scott came hurrying into the room. By that time everyone else in the ward was awake.

'Mrs Regan, what on earth's the matter with you?'

Mrs Regan was staring at her wide-eyed. She pointed to Edna's bed. 'There was a man,' she gasped. 'Under the bed . . . a doctor.'

Sister Scott looked across at Edna who was now weeping. 'Who was it, Mrs Curtis?'

Edna shook her head. 'I don't know,' she sobbed.

'It was a prowler,' Mrs Regan cried frantically. 'My God, we could have all been killed.'

'Just relax, Mrs Regan.' Sister stared thoughtfully across at Edna. 'We'll soon get to the bottom of this.'

'Gentlemen, it is with great pleasure that I announce the representative for this section.' Greg Mason held up the folded slip of paper he had just drawn from the basin and grinned around at the others. He unfolded the slip. 'And it's Doctor Craig Rothwell.' There was a cheer and a spattering of applause.

'Charming,' Craig groaned. He had thought these initiation games had been buried along with his college days. But no, Greg told him when he had mentioned this on his arrival in the staff common room where the new doctors were assembled, it was a tradition of the hospital. 'What do I have to do?'

Greg Mason was beaming at him. 'We haven't decided yet, but it has to be a test of courage, fortitude, and initiative – and one that will make those of all the other sections pale into insignificance.'

'And probably get us thrown out of the hospital.' Craig glanced at his watch; he had a stack of work to get through. 'Okay then,' he said with a sigh of resignation. 'Make it snappy. I've got work to do even if you haven't.'

Of course, they had it all worked out beforehand. 'There's a vicious rumour going around this hospital that Sister Scott wears long, old-fashioned bloomers,' Greg said with a quick glance around the table. He nodded to Craig. '*You* now have the honour of running the gauntlet over in the nurses' block, get into Scott's room then bring a pair of those long, old-fashioned bloomers across to Bunny's Place where we shall be eagerly awaiting your arrival. We will then hang those long, old-fashioned bloomers from the hospital flagpole.'

'And what if she *doesn't* wear long, old-fashioned

bloomers?' Craig pointed out.

'Then any bloomers at all. An article intimately worn by the said Sister Scott will have to do.'

Craig frowned around the table. 'Why pick on Sister Scott?' he wanted to know. 'I've got nothing against her.'

Greg Mason rolled his eyes heavenward. 'Your turn will come, never fear.'

'And, anyway,' Craig said, 'no one has ever managed to sneak into the nurses' quarters and lived to tell the tale – you know that.'

'Don't worry about that,' Greg said with a touch of smugness. 'We've got a foolproof plan.'

But Craig had to wait to learn what that foolproof plan was, because just then the subject of that plan walked determinedly into the room with a grim expression. Her gimlet eyes fixed on Craig. 'Doctor Rothwell,' she said in a voice that was like a whiplash.

'Yes, Sister?'

'Are you aware of the fact that you have a patient in my ward?'

'Patient?' Suddenly, he remembered. 'Mrs Regan.' He stood up quickly.

Sister Scott was regarding him coldly. 'Really, Doctor, this is too much,' she snapped. 'At your own request we prepared Mrs Regan for an examination. She's been suffering acute discomfort for almost fifteen minutes now.'

Craig could feel the warmth rising in his cheeks. 'I'm sorry, Sister, I forgot . . .'

'Did you indeed?' Sister Scott sniffed then

turned back to the door. 'If you're not back in that ward in three minutes, I'll report you.'

Flushed, embarrassed, painfully aware of the amusement that rippled quietly around him, he followed the Sister out of the room, quite prepared to bet on it that she really did wear long, old-fashioned bloomers that deserved to be run up the hospital flagpole where they could flutter proudly in the breeze for all to see.

'Then you'll arrange for my wife to give me that cheque?'

Grace Scott looked distastefully at the man she was quite certain had been hiding under Edna Curtis's bed the night before, and for whom the security people had scoured the hospital and grounds after she had raised the alarm. All they had found was a doctor's gown bundled up and thrust into the bushes near the side entrance.

'I'm afraid I can't do that, Mister Curtis,' she said flatly. 'The chequebook has been mislaid.' When she had reminded Edna Curtis earlier that morning that she still had her chequebook locked in her desk drawer, Edna had asked her to keep it there. She thought that would be safer; she was so forgetful at the moment that she would probably mislay it. But Grace knew there was more to it than that; she wanted to keep it from her husband who was now asking Grace to hand it over.

'Mislaid?' He was looking at her suspiciously.

'Lost.' Earlier she had received word from the Hospital Almoner that the hotel in which Frank and Edna Curtis had been staying since they arrived in the city had been in touch to advise that Frank Curtis had booked out of the hotel, leaving a suitcase that contained some of Edna's belongings. Sister Scott had arranged for the suitcase to be brought to the hospital. Edna had apologised for causing so much trouble. Grace had told her not to be so silly. Now, standing in a hospital corridor, surrounded by the usual activity of a busy city hospital, she was telling Edna's husband that Edna's chequebook had been lost. It wasn't true, of course. She remembered Edna's racing pulse when she had checked it the night before. 'We're hoping it will turn up, but for the time being . . .' she shrugged apologetically . . . 'I'm afraid we can't help you.'

Now Frank was beginning to turn nasty. 'Listen, lady,' he snarled. 'You've got that chequebook – and if I don't get it back, you're in for it.'

Sister Scott eyed him narrowly. If he could be so certain . . . 'How do you know I have the chequebook, Mister Curtis?' she asked deliberately.

Curtis hesitated. His eyes flickered along the corridor. 'I just know, that's all.'

Sister Scott studied him distastefully. 'That's interesting,' she said. 'Because the only person whom would I know I had the chequebook would be the man who was hiding in the Women's ward last night.'

Curtis glared back at her defiantly. 'I've just about had enough of you,' he growled.

Sister Scott remained calm. She knew how to

deal with people; she took no nonsense from them. 'And I've certainly had enough of you, Mister Curtis,' she returned icily. 'Now, if you don't get out of here and leave your wife alone, I will call the police and report you for terrorising the patients and staff of this hospital.'

Curtis bared his teeth in a smile that wasn't at all pleasant. 'You don't *know* the meaning of terror yet.'

'Are you threatening me?'

'No.' Curtis was still smiling. 'I'll go. I'll play it your way, Sister Scott.'

She watched him move back along the corridor towards the main entrance of the hospital. She knew she hadn't seen the last of him. She knew he meant trouble.

'Mrs Curtis, I think I should tell you I saw your husband again today,' she told Edna when she saw her that evening. She had just brought her some knitting which she had already started, and which Edna had offered to finish for her, grateful, she had said, for the opportunity, to keep her hands busy for the time she remained in the hospital. Grace was grateful, too. It seemed ages since she had started it; there just wasn't the time to settle down to it.

'Oh . . .' Edna was nervously fingering the knitting which Grace had given her along with the pattern. 'I'm sorry, Sister.'

She was always apologising; she felt she was causing so much trouble. 'He was asking for the chequebook. He was quite keen to have it.'

'It's my money, Sister.' Edna was staring up at her. 'It's all I have . . .'

'I understand,' Grace said with a nod. She felt so sorry for the woman. 'Anyway, we had words, and I had to order him out of the building.'

'Oh, Sister . . .' She was fearful again, a small frightened figure in a hospital bed. 'You shouldn't have done that. He can be so violent. If he's annoyed . . .'

'He doesn't worry me, Mrs Curtis.'

'Sister . . .' There seemed to be some great inner struggle raging within her. 'There's something I must tell you . . . . about my husband.' Grace Scott listened to her as she spoke, haltingly and in a nervous whisper that was at times almost inaudible, her hands resting on the knitting Grace had brought her. It was a story of violence and misery, of use and abuse. 'Every time I ran away, he found me and dragged me back,' Edna said unhappily. 'I thought, if we sold the property . . . it had been my father's, he had built it up . . . if we sold it we could start a new life somewhere, probably here in Sydney. But he demanded the money as his share of the sale, and when I refused he started drinking again. It got so bad that I just wanted to escape . . .' Her eyes were glistening as she stared up at Grace. 'I just wanted to die, Sister . . . and when he ran over that little boy . . . when he wouldn't stop . . . I just couldn't take any more.'

Sister Scott was suddenly alert. 'What little boy?'

'I think . . .' she sighed and shook her head . . . 'I don't know. Perhaps that little boy who was brought here . . . the doctor's son.'

'You mean, Doctor Denham's son?' Grace was leaning forward over the bed.

'Frank was yelling at me, and the little boy was standing at the side of the road. The car was heading straight for him. I screamed at Frank . . . and he swerved. But it was too late. I heard the bump. It . . . it was terrible. Frank just kept going. He wouldn't stop.' The tears were coming freely. Her voice was faint, uneven. 'He left me at the hotel, then went out . . . drinking. That's when I took those pills.'

'You realise you'll have to tell this to the police,' Grace said urgently.

'Yes, I realise that . . .' Abruptly, Edna's hand reached out and clutched Grace's arm. There was an imploring look in her eyes. 'Sister, you must keep away from him. Please. When he takes a dislike to someone . . . it affects him. He becomes . . . deranged.'

Craig Rothwell felt such a fool, dressed up as he was in a nurse's uniform one of the orderlies had dragged out for him from somewhere, a wig, and make-up, which was what Greg Mason's foolproof plan had turned out to be. Very good, very clever – dress up as a nurse and just sashay off into the nurses' quarters, no one would suspect a thing, he would be just another nurse returning to her room after a long and tiring day ministering to the sick. It was too ludicrous, too grotesque. The uniform was much too tight and the wig kept slipping. He wished he hadn't allowed himself to be talked into it. It was all too damned silly, anyway.

Covered by a sheet and flanked by the other young doctors who were only just managing, and not very successfully at that, to contain their amusement, he had been wheeled to the lift by the orderly who had been let in on the joke and who had obtained the nurses' uniform. 'Good luck,' Greg Mason had whispered as the lift doors had closed. The orderly had come up with him in the lift to the fourth floor where he was now all on his own, tottering along the corridor of the nurses' annexe, feeling such a fool, wishing he were out of it, but now, having come so far, determined to get it over with as quickly as possible.

Suddenly, he heard footsteps and voices coming along the corridor towards him. He looked around him in desperation. He could head back to the lift, but that had gone down again with the orderly and his trolley . . . No, that was no good. Then, seeing a coin-operated telephone on a shelf in a small alcove just ahead of him, he hurried towards it. As the two nurses passed him on their way to the lift, he had his back to them, apparently intent on a telephone conversation the major contribution to which was coming from the other end. He waited for some moments after they had gone before replacing the receiver then hurrying along the corridor to Sister Scott's room, the number of which Greg Mason, blast him, had told him repeatedly so he wouldn't forget and go blundering into the wrong room. Old-fashioned bloomers indeed.

The door was unlocked. Gently, he turned the handle, then eased the door open. The room was in darkness, as he had expected it would be; Sister Scott was still on duty, still patrolling the wards with her hawk-eye watchful for any sign of discrepancy. Craig closed the door gently behind him, then switched on the light.

He had taken only a couple of steps into the room, and was just registering to his surprise that all the dressing table drawers were open and there was clothing strewn across the floor, which was totally uncharacteristic for the Sister Scott he knew, when, suddenly, he was startled to hear a voice behind him.

'All right, Sister Scott.' It was a man's voice. 'Now you can give me that chequebook.'

Astonished, his heart pounding, Craig wheeled to face the man who was standing between him and the door. 'Who the hell are you?' he demanded, now full of righteous indignation that there should be an intruder in Sister Scott's room. 'What are you doing in this room?' It was then he noticed the gun in the man's hand, pointing directly at him.

The man was staring at him in growing bewilderment. 'Hey, you're not Sister Scott,' he said unnecessarily. 'You're . . . you're a bloke.'

A bloke dressed up in a nurse's uniform, wearing a wig, who was now staring at the gun in the intruder's hand. 'Whoever you are,' he commanded, with an assurance he didn't really feel, 'just put that gun down, and don't do anything stupid.' Turning, he moved to the telephone beside the bed.

'Don't do that!'

Craig had just lifted the receiver. Now, at the shrill peremptoriness of the man's tone, he replaced it.

'Now, look.' There was a wild look in the gunman's eye; Craig watched and waited for the opportunity to catch him off guard. 'There's no need for you to get uptight about this . . .' Then, as the man's eyes flickered, as he nervously ran his tongue over his lips, Craig, in his ill-fitting nurse's uniform, the wig – it was blonde and curly – tilting forward over one eye, sprang at him, catching him off balance, his hands reaching for his throat. The man stumbled beneath the force of Craig's weight as it cannoned against him. Craig also stumbled, his outstretched hand closing around thin air. There was a loud reverberating explosion, then a stinging sensation across one side of his face. He staggered. He raised his hand to touch his face where the stinging was becoming more intense. There was another explosion – a dull sound, really, quite flat – and then he was falling . . . and the shadows were closing in on him with frightening abruptness . . .

3

The head wound had been minor; it had required only a suture. But the second bullet had gone into his elbow, and that was more serious. It had disturbed the nerve structure and smashed some of the bone. Brian Denham didn't raise any false hopes. It looked as if the damage was permanent. 'In which case,' he told Craig, 'your arm will be permanently paralysed.'

The implications of that were stupefying. It meant that Craig's career as a surgeon was over before it had even properly begun. Just because of some silly prank which had brought him face to face with a gun-carrying lunatic; it was a bitter blow not only to him but would be to his father who had been bursting with pride that his son should have chosen to follow in his own illustrious footsteps. The only thing he could do now was resign.

'That's defeatist talk,' Jo Jo Adams said sternly. 'I don't like to hear defeatist talk.'

Jo Jo was his nurse. She was the sexy one. He had been snapping at her all day since Denham had broken the news about his arm. Then, realising what a pig he was making of himself, he had apologised to her. He had been giving his future a great deal of thought, he had told her. There was no choice for him now but to resign from the hospital. 'But you can still be a doctor,' she pointed out. 'There's more than one field in which you can specialise.'

He shook his head, then glanced down at the mug of tea he was holding in his left hand. 'It's not as easy as it looks.'

Jo Jo watched him as he awkwardly manipulated the mug. 'You'll manage.'

'Sure,' Craig said drily. 'Drinking tea is all right. But to perform surgery . . .'

'Who's to say?' Jo Jo was arranging a bunch of flowers in a vase beside the bed. She had told him she had pinched them from one of the private wards which was already looking like a florist's shop, anyway. 'So far, only Doctor Fredericks has said anything.'

It was Fredericks who had performed the operation on his elbow. He was reputed to be one of the best. 'You mean we wait for a second opinion?' He shook his head. 'Jo Jo, I'm a doctor . . .'

'An intern,' she corrected him, straightening and turning back to him from the flowers she had been arranging in the vase. 'I'm sorry, no offence meant, but you're just a new boy, Craig. You don't know it all yet.' She was regarding him very seriously. 'These guys . . . Fredericks, Shaw, Applewhite, Denham, Lindenmayer . . . they've been living the Hippocratic oath for years. You're just learning to spell it.' Craig smiled up at her. She was very pretty, very desirable, and if he wasn't feeling so down at the moment . . . 'You're crazy to think of handing in your resignation at this stage,' she went on. 'Hold off a bit. Don't be in such a rush.'

Craig was still smiling. Perhaps she was right. Perhaps he was being defeatist, too sorry for himself, making decisions before they were properly thought out . . . 'I must say, Nurse, you're doing wonders for my morale.'

'Of course,' she said, smiling back at him from the foot of the bed. 'Now, let's have no more of this defeatist talk, shall we? Let's just wait and see what happens.'

The police were still looking for Frank. They had asked her if she had any idea where he might be. But she didn't know where he could be. He had to be the man who shot that young doctor in Sister Scott's room. It couldn't have been anyone else.

'I'm sorry to worry you, Doctor, but I was wondering if you had any idea when I can leave. I'm much better now, and I don't want to take up valuable space when there's no need.

Jim Howard thought about this for a moment. 'Well, yes, basically, you *are* better,' he said. 'But we'd like to keep you here until the weekend at least. That's not so long, is it?'

Two days. 'No, it isn't.' She had been sitting in an easy chair at the end of the ward, trying to concentrate on a book, when the doctor had stopped to have a few words with her. She liked him; he had always been very friendly towards her. 'You've all been so kind,' she said warmly. 'I'll miss this place when I have to leave. But the thing is . . . it's just caused so much trouble, me being here . . . that young doctor being shot, and the police thinking it was Frank . . . I just feel so awful about it all.'

In the ward, Nurse Warner was holding a glass of water to the lips of an elderly woman patient who had just had a bout of violent coughing. Doctor Howard squatted down in front of Edna. He spoke quietly, earnestly. 'Mrs Curtis, you've been no trouble at all, believe me. If all our patients gave us as little trouble as you have, then a doctor's life would be pretty easy.' He patted her hand. 'You weren't to blame for anything that's happened,' he assured her. 'No one blames you, and there's no reason for you to blame yourself.' He pulled himself up onto his feet. 'Do you know where you'll be going when you leave the hospital?' he asked.

'Not yet,' she replied. She had thought about it a lot. 'But I'll find a place.' Somewhere – where she could be safe.

'How long have you been standing there?'

'I've just arrived.'

He had been dozing against the pillows when Laura came into the room. His lunch lay untouched on a tray beside his bed. Then, as if he had sense that she was watching him, he had stirred then opened his eyes. Laura nodded to the tray beside him. 'You haven't eaten your lunch.'

Craig glanced at the tray. 'No.'

'Are you feeling any better?'

He grimaced. 'I suppose the bad news has got around by now.' He touched the plaster on his right arm with his left hand.

'I was in Brian's office when Doctor Fredericks phoned through,' she told him. 'I'm so sorry, Craig.'

Craig laughed drily. 'I guess, in one way, I'm lucky that he was such a bad shot. Not that I'm much use as a surgeon without the use of one hand.'

Laura tried to sound encouraging. 'You're taking it very well.'

'Oh sure.'

Laura sat on the chair beside the bed. 'Doctor Shaw wants to conduct more tests on Toby.'

'How is he?'

Laura shrugged. There was still a long way to go yet. 'I seem to have started a whole chain reaction when I went out with you that night,' she observed unhappily. She looked up at him. 'Oh, I don't blame you. I blame myself.'

Craig's head was bandaged, his right arm heavily encased in plaster. He looked back at her. 'Why is it your fault?'

'Because . . .' there could be no question about it; she'd had plenty of time to reflect . . . 'I really wanted to go out with you that night. I was lonely, I needed company . . . companionship. But if I *hadn't* gone out with you, Toby wouldn't be here, perhaps Mrs Curtis wouldn't have tried to commit suicide, and her husband wouldn't have been waiting up in Sister Scott's room.'

'That's ridiculous, Laura.'

Laura shook her head sadly. A vicious circle of events. Brian had told her that it was more likely that Frank Curtis had been the driver of the car that had struck Toby. 'None of these things would have happened,' she said.

They sat in weighted silence for a few moments, Laura and the young doctor who had come within a fraction of losing his life because of her. 'How's Brian?' he asked finally.

'Busy.' She couldn't keep the bitterness out of her voice. At least Brian had his work. 'It's never been any other way. I suppose I'm being unfair.'

His bandaged head was turned on the pillow towards her. A trolley rattled along the corridor outside the room. 'I gather things aren't too good,' he remarked.

Laura smiled grimly. 'Well, they could be better.' There was always that silent reproach when she was with Brian. He didn't say much, but whenever he did, the reproach was there. Even in the way he looked at her sometimes. 'What will you do, Craig?'

'I'm packing it in.'

'You don't mean that.' Laura was shocked.

'I've had plenty of time to think about it.' Laura stared at him. They'd both had plenty of time to think. 'There must be something else I could do.'

Laura stood up. 'No, Craig,' she said. 'Don't even think about it. I've heard nothing but glowing reports about you. Brian said you had a brilliant career ahead of you as a surgeon.'

Craig smiled wrily. 'Interesting use of tense.'

'You know what I mean.'

'Forget it, Laura,' he said with a shake of his head. 'It's not up for discussion. As far as the medical profession goes, I *have* no future.'

And that was something else Laura could add to the list of things for which she could blame herself – and extra weight to a burden that was already intolerable.

A mecca – that was what Bunny Howard had hoped when he had opened his restaurant. Bunny's Place would be known far and wide as a place that sparkled and scintillated with wit and beautiful people, show business people, interesting people, who would come there and dine and smile at each other and draw up far-reaching plans over port and cigars. But instead of all that, instead of the glitter and the glamour, it seemed he had laid, as he put it, an A-grade egg.

'Come on, Dad,' Jim Howard chided him. 'Just because a chef let you down?'

Bunny Howard was extremely discouraged. His first-class place was turning out to be a no-class place. Even with his main clientele being drawn from the hospital across the road, he still had to have something to offer them. 'A string of chefs,' he said miserably. 'I fired the last one yesterday. The new bloke was supposed to start this morning.' And hadn't turned up. It was the last straw. It was enough to make a man turn to drink.

'So his grandmother's sick,' Jim said.

Bunny made a sound of disgust. His grandmother – what a lack of imagination. Bunny had heard it all before. A life of show business, of treading the boards the length and breadth of the British Isles and beyond had made him familiar with all the nuances. He looked woefully at his son, the doctor. Well, at least something in his life was working out, he thought. He was very proud of his son, the doctor. 'Let's face it, the food has been getting steadily worse for weeks now. I tell you . . .' he smiled tightly . . . 'it's so bad even *I* wouldn't eat here.' He noted his son's smile; Jim had always been a good audience, one of the best. 'I've had enough. I don't want to know any more.'

They were sitting at one of the tables, drinking coffee. It was already lunch time, and by now the place should have been busy. But Bunny had no chef, and because there was nothing he could offer his customers – what there were of them – he had kept the place closed. Scratching his moustache, he stared distractedly around the room which should, if his dreams for the place had been in any way realised, be bustling with celebrities by now. 'What will you do, Dad? If you have to sell?'

Turn back to the booze? It was tempting, drown all his woes – but he had promised . . . he shrugged and drank some more of his coffee. It was as if Jim had been reading his thoughts.

'I'll tell you, Dad,' he said seriously. 'If it's going to put you back . . .' he gestured towards the bar and the shelves of bottles behind it . . . 'then you'd better get rid of the place.' He looked intently at his father. 'Are you sure that's what you want to do?'

'Yes.' Absolutely sure. It just hadn't worked out, that was all. All those dreams he'd had of settling down one day and opening his own restaurant after so many agonising years of trying to make people laugh. Now no one was laughing. Bunny's Place. It and the rabbit were sinking without a trace.

Jim sat back in his chair with a sigh. 'All right then. We put it up for sale.'

'And the sooner the better,' Bunny said bitterly.

'Don't worry, Dad,' Jim said gently. 'It will work out. I guess it just wasn't meant to be.' Pushing back his chair, he stood up. 'I've got to get back now. I'm on Casualty. I'll come over as soon as I'm off duty. Okay?'

'Okay,' Bunny said expressionlessly.

Jim looked sympathetically down at his father. 'Why don't you have a lie-down in the meantime?'

'Don't worry, son,' Bunny said bleakly. 'I won't go back on the drink.'

'Mrs Denham?'

'Yes.'

'I'm Edna Curtis.' She had recognised the woman stepping out of the lift just as she was passing it. 'Could I talk to you?'

'Well . . .' Laura glanced about her uncertainly. 'I was just on my way to the Children's ward,' she said, and Edna experienced a pang. This was why she wanted to talk to her; there was something she desperately needed to explain.

'Please. I'll only keep you a moment.' She could tell that Laura Denham wasn't happy with the encounter. 'I'm so sorry about your little boy,' she went on quickly before the other woman had a chance to walk away from her which, from her expression, she clearly wished to do. 'I'd like to tell you how it happened, if I may.'

'It's not necessary,' Laura Denham said curtly, then, as she was about to turn away, hesitated. 'Yes . . . perhaps I *would* like to know how it happened.'

They had moved away from the lifts to the opposite wall of the corridor. 'I was in the car, so I'm partly to blame,' Edna began quietly. 'I begged my husband to stop. I begged him to go back, but he wouldn't listen to me.' Her voice broke as she relived those few ghastly moments again – the little boy about to cross the road, the sickening thud as the car struck him, and as she had swung back on the seat to stare in horror at the small, huddled figure lying motionless at the side of the deserted street, Frank pushing his foot down on the accelerator . . . 'I would give anything for it not to have happened . . . but it did and we're all suffering for it. I only wanted you to know . . .' she was losing control of herself; she turned away . . . 'I tried . . . I really did try . . . I'm so sorry . . .' With the tears welling in her eyes, she began to move back down the corridor towards the Women's ward.

'Mrs Curtis,' she heard Laura Denham calling after her. She stopped and turned back. 'I just wanted to say, thank you.' Edna gave her a shaky smile. Laura Denham walked up to her. 'Were you on your way back to the ward?'

'The doctors say I need to walk. I'm leaving at the weekend.'

Laura Denham was smiling at her. 'I'd be so grateful if you would have a cup of tea with me,' she said.

Edna knew that she was not being asked out of pity. She could see that the woman desperately needed to talk to someone. She could see how unhappy she was. 'Of course,' she said gratefully. 'I'd be very happy.'

When Jo Jo Adams saw the tall figure of Doctor Raymond Shaw waiting for the lift, she came to a quick decision. She hurried purposefully up to him. 'Excuse me, Doctor Shaw.'

He studied her appraisingly as she approached. She knew he had a reputation in the hospital as something of a ladies' man. 'Good afternoon, Nurse Adams,' he said in that rich, rolling voice of his. 'What can I do for you?'

'I'd like to ask you something.'

The charm exuded from him. 'Ask away, my dear.'

'It's about Doctor Rothwell.'

Shaw frowned thoughtfully. 'Yes, that was bad luck . . .'

'And I know I can't ask you to interfere with another doctor's patient without his knowledge . . .'

'Highly unethical.' Shaw nodded wisely.

'But could you talk to him at least?'

'About what?' He regarded her whimsically.

'One of the bullets smashed his right elbow,' she said. 'He's been told that the resulting nerve damage will leave his right hand useless.'

'Told by whom?'

'Doctor Fredericks.'

'Ah, yes . . .'

She knew she was taking a risk, that this wasn't the right way to go about things. 'He's very depressed, Doctor Shaw. To be a surgeon . . . that was his whole life. Now . . . She broke off as the lift arrived.

'No, go on,' Shaw said, ignoring the lift.

'He says he's going to resign from the hospital and give up medicine.'

The lift doors closed. 'Does he indeed?' Shaw was frowning again. 'Does his father know this?'

Jo Jo nodded. 'He's flying back from the Gold Coast.'

Shaw ran the palm of his hand over his jaw. 'Old Marcus won't be at all pleased by the news,' he observed.

'Then . . .' Jo Jo looked up appealingly into the eyes of the tall man with the closely cropped grey hair who was acknowledged to be one of the hospital's finest surgeons. 'Could you talk to him? I mean, I'm not suggesting you *examine* him, or anything . . .'

Which, of course, was exactly what she *was* suggesting. And Shaw knew it – she could tell by the amused glint in his deep-set eyes. 'Of course not,' he said. 'Where is he?'

'Third floor.'

Shaw glanced up at the indicator above the lift door, then took hold of Jo Jo's arm. 'We'll take the stairs,' he said, leading her off towards them.

Craig was surprised to see Dr Raymond Shaw. He was the last person he expected to see. He was even more surprised when Shaw asked Jo Jo Adams, who had come bustling into the room with him, to undress Craig's arm so he could have a look at the wound. 'Very dramatic goings-on,' Shaw remarked as he sat down beside the bed.

Craig nodded. Dramatic then, and strange now. He looked up at Jo Jo who was deftly stripping the bandages from his arm. 'That's a new dressing.'

'Yes, but rather sloppy,' Shaw said quickly. 'Needs rewinding.' He sat with his legs crossed. As usual, there was a carnation in his buttonhole. A picture of elegance, Shaw looked the part of a visiting specialist with a wealthy practice. He smiled at Craig. 'Bloomers, for heaven's sake. You might have thought of something a little more original. I pulled a similar stunt for my own initiation. That was over twenty years ago, mind you.'

'Yes, it was pretty silly,' Craig conceded. Jo Jo was still working on his arm.

'And most unfortunate, in your case.' Shaw nodded sympathetically. He was a man who could show marvellous sympathy, Craig had heard; his wealthy women patients simply adored him. 'I hear your father's on his way back.'

'Yes.' Craig wasn't looking forward to seeing his father; he knew how bitterly disappointed the old man would be.

'He won't much like this talk of your giving up medicine,' Shaw said seriously. Craig caught Jo Jo's eye as she stripped away the last of the dressing. She looked quickly away – rather guiltily, Craig thought. There was something very strange going on. Fredericks was the man who had operated on his arm; it wasn't Shaw's case at all. As Jo Jo stepped back from the bed with the dressing she had just taken from Craig's arm, Shaw leaned forward and began to closely examine the exposed wound. 'Try moving the little finger,' he said at last. Craig tried, but nothing happened. 'Now the index finger.' Again nothing happened.

'Would you like me to wait outside, Doctor?' Jo Jo asked.

'No need, Nurse,' Shaw replied, still thoughtfully examining Craig's arm. 'If we get caught, we get caught.'

So that was it; there was nothing official about this at all, no consultation with Fredericks, or with Denham – only with Jo Jo Adams who, Craig knew, was worried about him. She smiled nervously back at him when he looked at her in surprise.

Shaw picked up the large envelope he had brought into the room with him, and opening it, removed a set of X-rays. Placing the rest of them on the bed, he turned and held one up to the light. 'We borrowed them,' he explained, then glanced across at Jo Jo. 'It will be *your* responsibility to return them, Nurse.' He chuckled softly. 'We're in this together.' Lowering the X-ray, he turned back to Craig. 'How do you fancy the idea of a little more surgery on that arm?' he asked.

If there was a chance, a possibility . . . 'Do you think something can be done?'

'Well, at the risk of sounding egotistical . . .' He smiled compacently. 'What am I talking about? I *am* egotistical, and with every justification.' The smile faded. 'Yes, I think something can be done.'

Craig knew how dangerous too much hope could be. 'You mean, you think I could use the hand again?'

'It's possible.'

'What are the odds?'

'Oh . . .' Shaw thought about this for a moment. Craig watched him, not daring to hope for too much. 'Oh, I'd say seventy-thirty.'

'For or against?'

'Against.' Shaw motioned to Jo Jo to redress the wound.

'Who would operate? Doctor Fredericks?'

'I would.' Shaw slid the X-ray back into the envelope and stood up. 'That's if you trust yourself in my hands.'

Craig could se that he had no choice. The chances were seventy-thirty against the operation being a success – but at least the chances were there. 'I sure would.'

'Seventy-thirty,' Shaw reminded him.
Craig grinned up at him. 'I'll take it.'

4

Jim Howard had a brainwave. Of course! Why hadn't he thought of it before? All he needed to do now was convince his father.

'Come on, Dad. Have you ever met a country woman who *wasn't* a sensational cook? I'll take any kind of bet that she cooks like an angel.'

Edna Curtis was leaving the hospital that morning. She had no place to go, she had no job – no prospects, really – and here, Jim suddenly realised, she could have both of those things. Bunny needed a cook, was having all sorts of trouble finding one . . .

'Look, son,' Bunny said wearily. 'I swore I'd never employ another female after that Davenport woman – and I won't change my mind.'

'But Edna Curtis is nothing like that Davenport woman,' Jim insisted.

Bunny gestured in disgust. 'Nor was that Davenport woman like the Davenport woman when she arrived for the interview. There, I said when I first set eyes on her – that woman is a saint, believe me. With her, there would be no problems – a thoroughly capable human being, I told myself.' He gave a brief, mirthless laugh. 'Within three days, I was tripping over empty Scotch bottles, and was beaten up when I tried to kick those two sailors out of her room.'

'That was the Davenport woman,' Jim reminded him. 'I'm talking about the Curtis woman. Besides, what have you got to lose? You've sacked eight cooks since you started this place. Come on, Dad.' He put his arm around his father's shoulder; he really did want Edna Curtis to get this job; he was sure she would make a success of it. 'Give her a chance.'

Bunny sighed. 'Okay, Doctor,' he said. 'But the first time she puts a foot wrong, out she goes.'

Jim Howard gave his father a fond hug. 'Thanks, Dad,' he said happily. 'You've got a heart of gold.'

It was dark in the staff car park, as reaching in her bag for her keys, Grace Scott hurried across the asphalt towards her car. She was already late; she had promised to pick up Helen Gordon at seven-thirty, and it was now past that. They had promised themselves an evening out on the town. They were both looking forward to it.

Above her was the hospital and its rows of lights. She could make out her car ahead of her, standing at the far end of the car park where it was fringed with trees and shrubbery.

She had the key ready by the time she reached the car. She slid it into the lock. Suddenly hearing a sound behind her, she was turning when a shadowy figure leapt out at her from among the trees and slammed her hard against the side of the car. A hand clamped over her mouth, stifling her scream. She began to struggle wildly. She kicked and twisted, she tried to lash out with her arms, but the man was too powerful; he was forcing her back against the car. In the gloom of the car park, she could only just make out his features thrusting towards her, gleaming and distorted with hatred. In her panic, she struggled more fiercely. Then she felt something cold and sharp pricking her throat. She stopped struggling, and stared helplessly at her attacker.

'My, my,' Frank Curtis muttered thickly. 'We *have* got ourselves tarted up tonight, haven't we?' His body was trapping her against the car. She tried to dodge to one side, but the pricking sensation against her throat intensified slightly. She knew he was holding a knife against her throat. Her body sagged. 'One peep out of you,' Curtis hissed, 'and I'll slit your throat.'

Still holding the knife against her throat, his hand still over her mouth, he dragged her roughly away from the car towards the bushes just behind it. 'Okay,' he muttered. 'I want to get in to see my wife . . . so you tell me . . . what's the best way?' The reek of liquor on his breath made Grace feel nauseous. He took his hand from her mouth. 'I warn you . . .'

Grace glanced nervously down at the dull gleam of the knife poised now less than an inch from her throat. 'She's gone.'

The blade jerked. 'What do you mean – gone?'

'She left the hospital this morning.'

'Where is she?' he demanded.

If she knew, she would probably tell him. 'I don't know,' she gasped. 'Please . . .'

He clamped his hand over her mouth again. She could see the glint of his teeth as he leered at her. 'You've been a real pain in the neck to me, haven't you?' There was a dangerous edge to his voice. 'You've caused me nothing but trouble.' The knife blade was almost touching her throat again. 'So high and mighty . . . well then, let's see just what *is* under all that clean efficiency . . .'

Jim Howard brought her into the hospital through a side entrance where there was less chance of running into anyone. He led her to one of the private examination rooms on the ground floor.

'Where are you going?' she asked weakly as, having made sure she was comfortable, he turned back to the door.

'I'm going to arrange for you to be examined. Then I'm calling the police.'

'No.' He was surprised by the sharpness of her tone.

He had found her in the car park, dishevelled, her dress torn, her face streaked with dirt and tears. He had just left the hospital and was taking a short cut across the car park when he had heard someone whimpering in the shadows. 'Look, Sister, something very serious happened out there.' She had told him it was Curtis; she had been quite hysterical when he found her. 'The man's a maniac. His wife almost committed suicide because of him, and he shot a doctor in this hospital.' She had to see that there was no alternative than to call the police.

'Please, Jim . . .' She was shaking her head from side to side. 'No.'

Crossing the room, he sat on the bed beside her. 'We've worked together too long for me not to understand you,' he said reasonably. 'You would be the first person to have that man arrested and charged. But you won't do it. Why?'

Grace Scott was staring straight ahead of her. 'Would you mind calling Helen Gordon and asking her to come over here?'

'Very well.' Jim rose to his feet.

She looked bleakly up at him. 'And I don't want you telling anyone about this.'

This was something she had been insisting from the moment he had discovered her in the car park. 'I won't say anything,' he said tightly. 'But I do think we're making a terrible mistake. He's done it once. He could do it again – and I'm helping you protect him.'

'Please call Helen,' Grace Scott said distantly, staring straight ahead of her again.

But Helen Gordon, when she arrived about half an hour later, couldn't persuade her to change her mind. 'But that's ridiculous,' she protested. 'The police *have* to be called.'

'Please, Helen,' Grace said wearily. 'I don't want to go over it all again.'

Jim Howard stood by the doorway and watched them. He had asked Helen when she arrived to try and talk some sense into Sister Scott. Helen was doing her best. 'I can't *believe* you're saying this. After what that man did to you.'

'Helen . . .' Grace Scott's eyes filled with tears. 'I asked you to come here to help me . . . not give me a lecture.'

'But the police will arrest him,' Helen persisted. 'They'll stop him doing the same thing to someone else.'

Grace was weeping now. She held a handkerchief to her eyes and wept. 'I know they should be called,' she sobbed. 'I *know* that. But I will *not* put myself in the position of being questioned . . . not in the way they have to question women who have . . . have been in the same situation. I've seen it happen . . . here, in this hospital. They have to do it . . . ask questions . . .' she shook her head woefully . . . 'but not to me. I won't *let* it happen.'

Later, much later, in her room, over coffee, she told her friend, Helen Gordon, why she was so insistent about not reporting the matter to the police. It had happened once before, back home in Perth, when she had been a student nurse, bright-eyed and trusting, quite innocent.

'I was on my way home one night, and these two men . . . they attacked me. I reported them to the police, and they were arrested in a matter of hours. And then . . . then everything started to go wrong for me. These men insisted I had encouraged them . . . a shudder went through her . . . 'that I'd actually consented. You wouldn't believe the questions the police asked me, Helen. Then, in the court, it was even worse. Well, to cut it short, those two men were acquitted. I couldn't prove anything, you see. The most incredible thing, Helen, was the change in my own family. They were outraged by what had happened. They knew I was innocent, but somehow . . . I felt they blamed me for letting it happen. I could see it in their eyes . . . the reproach. They were a very straitlaced family. Through no fault of my own, I had disgraced them. Finally, it got so bad that I packed my bags and left home. I left town. I never went back.' She began to cry. 'I know it's wrong not to go to the police, but I just couldn't face it, Helen. The humiliation . . .' She shook her head in determination. 'I will *not* go through it again.'

If the operation was supposed to be such a success, as everyone was saying it was, then why was he still unable to move his hand? But Denham was insisting the operation *had* been a success; he had the X-rays to prove it. There was no *physical* reason why Craig couldn't move his hand.

'Oh great,' Craig groaned. 'So now it's all psychosomatic.'

Denham shrugged. 'You know from your own studies of the musculo-skeletal system that the symptom frequently carries an unconscious thought content . . .

Craig shook his head in bewilderment. The disappointment when he had discovered he still couldn't use his hand had been acute. He had taken to snarling at Jo Jo Adams again. 'I can't *believe* all this is happening to me,' he wailed. 'One moment I'm being convinced that the operation has been a success. Now I'm being subjected to psychotherapy.'

'You'll be subjected to *nothing* against your will, Doctor,' Denham said tartly.

Bunny and Bert – now *there* was a combination. As a song and dance team they had closed more theatres than any other double act. When they split up, Bert Singleton had gone to America while Bunny had come to Australia where he was doing quite nicely, thank you, closing up his restaurant without any help at all.

No, that was wrong. He did have help now – and he had to admit, despite his earlier reservations about employing another woman who might go tripping along the same primrose path as had La Davenport of no fond memory, that it was working out quite well. Okay, so he had been proved wrong. Edna Curtis was no Davenport. She was turning out to be very useful. Already she was almost taking charge. He was telling her about Bert Singleton – the other half of the Bunny and Bert theatre-closing combination – who had just written to him from America. His daughter was coming to Australia – and that was another problem.

Abbie Singleton was a top singer in the States. She had made a number of albums, had been on television, she had a big following, not only in the States but in Australia as well. 'I'm sure you'll have a chance to meet her,' Edna said.

'Meet her?' Bunny was puffing on a cigar. He eyed her unhappily. 'I'll be doing more than just meeting her. You see, I wrote to Bert about six months ago, telling him about my restaurant here and what a huge success it was. Now he's talking about her doing some cabaret here in the restaurant while she's here. A favour, he said.' Cigar smoke swirled around his head. 'Some big favour,' he added gloomily.

'But that's just what this place needs,' Edna said brightly. 'The people would pour in to hear her.'

'Sure, they would pour in. She's a star. Of course they would. But it's too late. I've just been going through the latest stack of bills. I can't get anything more from the bank – and if this place is going to survive, it needs thousands of dollars injected into it.' He shook his head sadly. 'I'll drop Bert a note and see if I can wriggle out of it.'

Edna was frowning thoughtfully. She seemed to be reaching for a decision. 'Five thousand dollars,' she said at last.

Bunny took the cigar from his mouth and blinked at her from behind his spectacles. 'Five thousand dollars?'

'I mean, would it be enough?'

'Where would I get five thousand dollars?' he asked tolerantly.

'From me,' she replied. 'It's the money I had left after I paid all the debts on my property. I'd be happy to invest it in your restaurant.'

Bunny studied her through the cigar smoke.

Five thousand would be very useful, of course. He shook his head sorrowfully. 'That's kind of you, Edna, but I couldn't accept it. Thanks all the same. I really do appreciate the offer. I'm sorry.'

'But why not? You need the money. You just told me so.'

'It's just that I have my reasons for not wanting you to invest in this place.'

'What reasons, Dad?'

'Reasons? Yes, well . . .' Bunny had just returned from the markets. Jim had helped him unload the van. 'Well . . . reasons.' Bunny was obviously uncomfortable.

Jim had been surprised when Edna had mentioned the offer she had made to Bunny the day before. Five thousand dollars was a lot of money. Edna had told him it was all she had, but she had known they could have made a go of the place – her and Bunny – if it was enough to get Jim's father out of the red. She had thought that, by helping him, she would become some kind of minor business partner. She hadn't wanted to upset him.

'Look, Dad, you've been running around, begging for a loan – and when someone offers you one, the least you can do is explain why you're refusing it.' He thought of something. 'It's nothing to do with . . . well, you know . . . the attempt she made on her life, is it?'

'No, Jim,' Bunny returned quickly. 'Nothing like that at all. It's . . .' He hesitated. 'Okay. I know I've been trying to borrow money,' he went on. 'Because I've been kidding myself that more money could make this place work. If a stranger had coughed up . . . sure, I would have grabbed it. But when Edna offered me her own money, I realised she would just be throwing good money after bad. I thought she'd had enough trouble in her life without me adding to it.'

Edna was chopping up vegetables in the kitchen. Jim called her across to the table where he and Bunny were drinking coffee. When she came, rather hesitantly and with an apprehensive expression, he invited her to sit down. He turned back to his father. 'I go along with Edna as far as this place is concerned,' he said. 'She thinks it has a future, if it's run properly, and I seriously think you should reconsider her offer of a loan.'

Bunny glanced quickly at Edna, then shrugged. 'Edna, the trouble is that I'm a lousy businessman. You must have already noticed that.'

'Yes, I've noticed that,' Edna said drily.

Bunny smiled ruefuly. 'A song and dance man – that's me. A few jokes. I got out at the right time.'

'But if you let Edna run the place,' Jim suggested to his father, 'and you simply handle the front of the house, I would say you'd be both on a winner.'

Bunny's eyes widened behind his spectacles. 'You mean, Edna would be the boss?'

'You've just been saying what a lousy businessman you are,' Jim pointed out to him. 'A song and dance man who got out at the right time.'

'Not the boss,' Edna said. 'A junior partner who

would do everything she could to make the business work for you.'

Jim was leaning forward across the table, staring at his father. 'But to make it work, Edna will have the say as to who gets credit in future and how much you pay for food.' He sat back in his chair. 'That sort of thing.'

'I'd still like to think it over.' Bunny pushed his chair back and stood up.

Jim winked at Edna. He was sure the old man would see the sense in the arrangement. If he didn't, well then a little more pressure would have to be applied. He would come around in good time. He also stood up after draining what was left in his cup. He was on duty in a few minutes.

They stood around Craig's bed, trying to convince him that he could be made to move his arm again if only he would agree to submit to the course that had already been outlined to him. Doctor Thornton, who had developed this particular course, had had considerable success with it in the past. Marcus Rothwell had already cited to Brian Denham one example of that success. He had watched him using his new drug on a sailor who had been paralysed after an explosion at sea. He had re-created the entire incident, and when it came to the point when the ship went down, Thornton had made the fellow swim for his life. He had woken up quite cured. Now they were suggesting something similar with Craig Rothwell. 'Let's hope it worked,' Brian Denham had said to

Craig's father who had just flown in from the Gold Coast. 'You see, there's also the problem of convincing Craig that it *is* psychosomatic.'

'You'll forgive me if I'm sceptical, Doctor,' Craig said when the course was suggested to him.

Marcus Rothwell nodded. 'That's understandable, son, after the disappointment of the second operation. But Doctor Thornton here has had a lot of success with this particular treatment.'

'All right then,' Craig said after reflecting on this for a few moments. 'I guess we've got nothing to lose.'

The nurse gave him an injection of Doctor Thornton's drug. 'He'll ramble on a bit,' Thornton explained to Denham and the older Doctor Rothwell. 'But the important thing is to regress him to before the shooting. When he *knew* he could move his hand.'

The drug was quick to take effect. Looking down at Craig, Denham could see that he was beginning to lose his grasp of what was going on around him. Taking a pencil torch from his pocket and switching it on, Thornton leaned forward and directed its light onto Craig's eyes. 'Craig,' he said slowly, carefully, as the others watched in interest, 'I want you to concentrate on that point of light . . . concentrate . . . let it fill the world. It's bright . . . bright . . . you need to close your eyes . . .' he held the torch steady in front of Craig's eyes . . . 'close your eyes . . .' Craig closed his eyes . . . 'now look upwards. You can't open your eyes now, Craig,' he went on after a brief pause. 'You can't open them . . . and now your arms are heavy . . . heavy . . .' Taking Craig's left arm, he raised it, then let it fall over the side of the bed. Craig lay very still; he looked perfectly relaxed. 'Can you hear me, Craig?'

'Yes . . .'

Thornton was leaning over him again. 'You've just arrived from Melbourne . . .'

'Mmmmm . . .'

'You're coming to work at this hospital . . .'

'Mmmmm . . .' Craig's voice was coming from very far away . . . 'surgeon . . . can't any more . . . the hand . . .'

'But this is *before*, Craig . . . before the shooting . . .'

'Ah . . .'

'When you could still move your hand . . .'

'Ah . . . hand offends thee . . .' he gave a short, strangled laugh . . . 'Sunday school . . . hand offends thee, cut it off . . .' He laughed again. Thornton glanced up at Denham, who shrugged, then at Marcus Rothwell, who also shrugged. 'Deserved what it got . . . old hand . . .'

'You can move it, Craig,' Thornton said persuasively.

'Crook the finger . . . women come running . . . Laura did . . . Brian's a nice guy . . . why . . .' His voice trailed away. Suddenly tense at the mention of Laura's name, Denham stared at him.

'You can move the hand, Craig,' Thornton persisted. 'Getting in a car . . . turn the ignition, Craig.'

'Getting in a car . . .' Craig was frowning in concentration. Brian Denham stood very still. What was it he had said about Laura? Come running?'

'That's right, Craig.'

'With Laura . . .' There it was again. 'Getting in the car with Laura . . . we stayed out all night . . . then little boy gets hit because hand . . . hand offends . . . Laura . . . me . . . no good . . .'

Brian Denham felt the coldness spreading inside him. If what Craig was saying . . . but of course it was true, it had to be true. Having succumbed to Thornton's new drug, there was no restraint. As the cold, implacable hatred built up inside him, Denham turned away, no longer able to bear the sight of the man who had spent the night with his wife. The dreadful silence in the room was broken by Craig's faint, listless monotone.

'Cut it off . . . hands that . . .'

Hands that what? Caressed his wife? Denham's hands clenched by his sides. Yes, that was what he meant. Behind him, Thornton was working on Craig again.

'Craig . . . before all that . . . back in Melbourne . . . coming to your flat . . . you take out your keys . . .'

'Keys . . .'

'You put the key to your flat in the lock . . .'

'Ah . . .' Craig was frowning again.

'Show me how. Pick out the right key and put it in the lock.'

Denham turned back to face the bed, as, slowly,

Craig's right hand began to move, rising from the counterpane where it had been lying, his fingers going through the motions of selecting a key from the bunch he believed he was holding in his hand, taking the key – the right one – and inserting it in the lock, turning it . . . He made it seem so easy. Thornton grinned up at the two men behind him. Denham's expression remained grim. Thornton turned back to Craig.

'Now . . . listen to me carefully, Craig . . . when you wake up, you'll still be able to move your hands, turn keys, tie sutures . . . make incisions . . . all those things . . . there's nothing wrong with your hand, Craig . . . it's perfectly normal . . . it functions . . . when you wake up . . . Now!'

Everyone standing around the bed watched Craig as he blinked rapidly a number of times, the focused on each of them in turn. Then, puzzled, he was looking at his hand, still raised from the bed, still poised as if he were about to fit an imaginary key into an imaginary look. He giggled wildly; he was still partially under the effect of Doctor Thornton's drug. 'I really *can* move it.'

Marcus Rothwell was beaming down at his son. 'Of course you can, my boy. You can be operating again in a month.'

Craig was giggling again. Denham couldn't take any more of it. His bitterness was choking him.

'Son, is there anything between you and Laura Denham?'

It was an odd question. Craig looked up at his

father with a slight frown. 'No. Why?'

'When you were hypnotised, you talked about Laura . . . and yourself . . . and about their son's accident. You were blaming yourself. You said you stayed out all night.'

My God, Craig thought in dismay – and what else might he have said if they had let him go on? Would he have gone on to tell them about the motel room? And Brian Denham had been there to hear everything he said. 'She stayed out all night,' he said dismally. 'I took her to dinner the night before the accident. She kicked on after I left. The boy went looking for her and was hit by the car. Yes, I guess I *do* blame myself.' He didn't like having to tell a lie, but there was nothing else for it. He could move his hand again, but had come very close to revealing what had happened between Laura and himself to the audience of eminent doctors, one of whom was his father and another the husband of the woman who had deceived him.

'Is that all?' His father was regarding him quizzically.

'That's all. Have I ever lied to you?'

Marcus Rothwell smiled faintly. 'Yes.'

'That's all there is, Dad,' Craig insisted, aware that his father still didn't quite believe him.

'I'll be here until this evening,' Marcus Rothwell told his son. 'If there's anything you want to tell me . . .'

Craig shook his head in exasperation. 'That's all there is,' he said obstinately.

The thought that Brian Denham would be along

at any moment to demand an explanation made him apprehensive. He had no doubt at all that Denham *would* come, *would* ask him to explain himself – and when he did come, just as Raymond Shaw was telling him that with some physiotherapy, heat and ultra wave, as well as some honest work on his part, he would be able to use his hand properly again in no time at all, Craig was ready for him. He had already made up his mind not to dodge the issue if it were placed squarely in front of him.

'Apparently I said some things when I was under hypnosis,' he said after Shaw had gone and Denham was watching him bleakly from the foot of his bed.

'Yes,' Denham said thinly. 'About staying out all night with my wife.'

'I'm sorry,' Craig murmured, holding the other man's gaze.

'I've yet to know what it is you have to be sorry about.' Denham stood there with his arms folded, his expression severe. 'Am I to be the last person in the hospital to know?' He shook his head. 'It doesn't help my position here, you know.'

Stung by his admonitory tone, Craig snapped, 'Maybe if you had thought less about your position here and more about your marriage, this wouldn't have happened.'

Denham studied him coldly. 'If I'm to be blamed for it, perhaps you should tell me what *did* happen.'

There it was – the direct challenge. 'I knew you

would be coming,' Craig said after a moment's hesitation, 'and it seems to me that you should know.' He took a deep breath preparatory to the plunge. 'The night before your son was hit by the car . . .'

'Laura and you . . ?' Now there was sick certainty in Denham's eyes. Craig felt sorry for him. He nodded.

'Yes, and it was my fault. I knew she was lonely. I knew she was unhappy . . . and I should have backed away. Maybe I'm just too used to taking whatever I want.' Now he was being painfully honest; he wasn't trying to excuse himself in any way. 'Anyway, I did. It wasn't Laura's fault. It was my fault entirely.' Denham said nothing. 'So don't blame her,' Craig continued. 'She was lonely . . . because she loved you. She was unhappy . . . from love of you.'

The silence stretched. Finally, Denham said, with a curt nod, 'Thank you, Doctor, for telling me the truth at last. But, in future, when you speak to me – and that will be when you cannot avoid it – you will not use the word 'love'. It's a good word – and you hear it from your mouth – it makes me ill.'

Unhappily, Craig stared after him as he wheeled and left the room. There was nothing for him to say.

5

'Any allergies of which you are aware?'

'Oh, I sometimes feel a little funny after I've had a drink. Fuzziness in the morning.'

'That's called a hangover.'

Mrs Lawson was Raymond Shaw's patient. 'Gall bladder,' he had told Gail Henderson. 'Tiny bit neurotic. Needs handling.' He had asked Gail to conduct more tests on his patient on whom he would be operating the following day.

Mrs Lawson was a large, cheerful woman. Now she was frowning. 'I'm sure I've never had a hang-over,' she said thoughtfully. 'I've read about the enzymes in red wine, and apparently, I'm a special case.'

'If you say so, Mrs Lawson,' Gail said. 'Now, the background to your present condition . . .'

'Pains.' Mrs Lawson grimaced. Before, when Shaw had teased her, she had simpered and blushed; dimples had appeared in her cheeks. 'I thought my appendix had grown again.' She looked inquiringly up at Gail. 'Is that possible?' Gail smiled patiently and shook her head. 'That's what dear Doctor Shaw said. I was thinking I would end up in the text books.'

'And so you may, Mrs Lawson . . .'

'I really do feel sick some mornings,' Mrs Lawson said unhappily.

'You've had tests for pregnancy?' Gail asked her.

Mrs Lawson looked appalled. 'It can't be that.'

'It's not an uncommon condition.'

'At my age?' Gail guessed her to be in her early forties. 'Doctor Henderson, you flatter me.' Gail was certain that Doctor Shaw flattered the woman all the time; she was undoubtedly one of his more wealthy patients. 'Anyway, Doctor Shaw tied my tubes years ago.' She had a sudden thought. '*They* can't grow again, can they?'

'If they have,' Gail assured her, 'then you'll most certainly be in the text books.' She made a note on the clipboard she was holding. 'Do you and Doctor Shaw have a long operating acquaintance?'

'He's very understanding,' Mrs Lawson replied with a nod.

'This nausea . . . is it always after a party?' Then, as Mrs Lawson looked at her blankly, 'Have you always been out the night before?'

'But I'm not out every night of the week.' Mrs Lawson showed her surprise. 'Oh, we sometimes entertain, of course. I assure you, I lead a perfectly normal life.'

'Yes . . .' Gail tapped her pen lightly on the clipboard. 'So we've got nausea, pains like appendicitis . . .'

'I sometimes don't eat until late,' Mrs Lawson supplied. 'After the theatre, when we go out, something like that . . .'

When the results of the tests on Mrs Lawson came back from the laboratory, Gail was worried; they were not as she had expected them to be if it were simply a gall bladder that needed removing. She called the laboratory and asked if they wouldn't mind running them through again, which only confirmed the original results. There was something radically wrong.

'You mustn't operate on Mrs Lawson tomorrow.' She had tracked Shaw down to the staff common room. 'I've just had the results of the tests . . .'

'Gail, darling,' Shaw smoothly interrupted her. 'I've also had tests done on her. I just wanted you to carry out some more so that she would be pleased by all the attention she was receiving.'

Gail was appalled. 'But you *can't* do that operation.'

'The lady's in pain,' Shaw pointed out offhandedly. 'Tomorrow morning . . .' he made a scissoring motion with two fingers . . . 'snip, snip, gall bladder out, no more pain. Then she'll have to find her symptoms somewhere else in her body. Now, if you'll excuse me . . .'

He was turning away when Gail grabbed his arm. 'She could have intermittent porphyria,' she said.

'I see.' Shaw nodded wisely. 'Young doctor syndrome, is it? You've been reading too many textbooks. Yes, the symptoms *can* look similar. It's just that in twenty-five years of practice I've seen only three cases of porphyria – and I don't know *how* many thousand cases of gall bladder. I can assure you, my dear,' he went on patronisingly, 'it's not porphyria.'

'But if it *is*,' Gail persisted, 'she could die under anaesthetic.'

Shaw's patience suddenly deserted him. 'Now listen here, young woman,' he said tautly, 'I've performed surgery on Mrs Lawson before. She didn't die then, and she won't die now. So let's hear no more of that kind of dangerous talk. I've already made my diagnosis, and that's final.'

If Raymond Shaw wouldn't listen to her, then perhaps Mrs Lawson would. As Gail saw it, it was imperative that the operation not be performed until it had been established without a doubt that Gail's guess as to the true meaning of her symptoms was established. She had to see Mrs Lawson and put the case to her.

'Mrs Lawson, I have to say a few things,' she said some minutes later after she had let herself into the woman's room, 'and I'm most reluctant to say them.'

She realised, as soon as the words were out, that it was the wrong approach. She had only succeeded in frightening the woman. 'What's the matter? Is there something wrong? Am I sick, or . . ?'

'You wouldn't be here if you *weren't* sick,' Gail reminded her. 'The question is – *why* are you sick?'

Mrs Lawson was still looking frightened. 'Gall bladder. I've been martyred to it.'

'But that's it, you see,' Gail said quickly. 'I'm not sure it *is* your gall bladder.'

Puzzled, Mrs Lawson frowned up at her. 'But Doctor Shaw . . .'

'Doctor Shaw asked me to do these extra tests. Now they indicate that your troubles may be . . . may lie elsewhere.'

'But Doctor Shaw . . .'

'Doctor Shaw is very busy at the moment,' Gail told her. 'He feels the original tests were sufficient . . .'

Mrs Lawson's mouth was working. 'Then why did I have to have a second set?'

Gail cleared her throat. She wasn't finding this easy. 'Sometimes we like to double-check, to make absolutely sure.' She tried another tack. 'Let me put it this way, Mrs Lawson. There's a small chance that your trouble is *not* gall bladder. Doctor Shaw feels it is what he originally said it was . . .'

'And you disagree?' Mrs Lawson broke in, then when Gail nodded, added shrewdly. 'He's much more experienced, of course.'

There was no doubt of that. 'But he hadn't had a chance to look at the results of the second test. And he operates tomorrow.'

In the silence that followed, Mrs Lawson stared up at her in growing doubt before saying, in a small voice, 'What if you're right?'

'There could be complications,' Gail replied. Now it was time to come to the point. 'Doctor Shaw won't listen to me. The only person who could stop the operation is you.'

There was another long silence. Mrs Lawson was slumped back against the pillows, looking quite panic-stricken. 'I shouldn't have to make that decision,' she said at last. 'Doctors are supposed to make these decisions.'

'It's your . . .' Gail just managed to stop herself from using the word 'life' . . . 'health, Mrs Lawson.'

'My husband,' Mrs Lawson exclaimed weakly. 'We should be talking to my husband.'

'Where is your husband?'

'In London. On business.'

'Then it has to be up to you alone.'

Now Mrs Lawson was looking throroughly confused. 'But I can't tell Doctor Shaw I won't have the operation. He'll think I'm a fool.'

Better to be thought a fool than . . . 'If I'm right, the complications could be quite serious,' Gail informed her.

The panic was back again, more marked now. 'Are you saying I could . . . die?' she asked fearfully. Gail didn't answer; she didn't think she needed to answer. She suspected that this was the first real decision the woman had faced in more years than she cared to remember. Mrs Lawson sighed distractedly. 'I honestly don't know which is the harder – dying or being made to look a fool.'

'I know which *I'd* prefer,' Gail said quietly.

'That's all right for *you* to say,' Mrs Lawson yelped. 'And what if you're wrong, and Doctor Shaw is right?'

'Then we'll both look fools,' Gail answered simply.

The well-groomed and polished Doctor Raymond Shaw had lost his poise. At first, he thought it was a case of last-minute nerves, and had tried to reassure her that everything would be all right, and that she would have to have the operation because if she didn't the pain would only become worse. She was in good hands, he had told her; the very best. Then, when she had persisted, he had accused her, his good nature now touched with a hint of acerbity, of being silly. Then he had become suspicious.

'Has Doctor Henderson been talking to you?'

'I don't want to get anyone in trouble . . .'

'Then she has.' Mrs Lawson nodded. She was one of his best patients; God only knew how many organs he had removed from that overweight body of hers. Now someone who had no right to do so was interfering and making life difficult. 'Doctor Henderson is young and inexperienced,' he said tightly. 'This is a training hospital, and Doctor Henderson is here for training. She's here to learn from senior surgeons such as myself.' He was doing his best not to show his anger. He spoke quietly, reassuringly. 'I asked her to do the second run of tests on you as a favour to her – to broaden her experience. But she has overstepped her brief. She has abused my trust.' He patted his patient's shoulder and gave her one of his famous smiles. 'Now just relax. We'll do this operation tomorrow, and there'll be no more pain.'

But Mrs Lawson wasn't reassured. She had become quite determined. 'I won't have the operation until more tests have been done,' she stated firmly.

That was what she wished; it was her last word on the subject. Raymond Shaw was furious. Of all the interfering, all the damned cheek . . . there was only one answer for it. Doctor Gail Henderson had to go. He would make sure of it.

'Doctor Shaw has made a very serious complaint,' Brian Denham said. 'He tells me you came between him and his patient . . . Mrs Lawson . . . and that you said things to Mrs Lawson that were derogatory of Doctor Shaw's competence as a surgeon.'

Gail sat in front of the desk in the Medical Superintendent's office, feeling quite chilled at the formality with which Denham was addressing her. Shaw himself was sitting at one side of the desk, his arms folded, his legs crossed, looking quite relaxed. Denham regarded her sternly. Let them get it over with, Gail thought defiantly; let them drum her out of the place – but she wouldn't go with her head bowed. Now Denham was asking her a direct question. 'Did you tell Mrs Lawson to withdraw permission for her operation tomorrow?'

Perhaps she had tackled this in the wrong manner. If she had brought the test results directly to Brian Denham who, as Medical Superintendent, would undoubtedly have found a way around the impasse, it might have been better. But, because she liked Raymond Shaw, she hadn't wanted to make trouble for him. She had just thought that by persuading Mrs Lawson to withdraw her permission, he would have time to study the test results more closely. Now, because she *had* been able to persuade Mrs Lawson, they were after her blood. 'Yes,' she said.

'Why?'

'Because I felt the operation would endanger her.'

Denham cast a quick, worried glance at Shaw, then looked back again at Gail. 'Why did you think that?'

Gail placed the folder she had brought with her on the desk. The results were all there. When she told him so, Denham drew the folder towards him. 'You took these on whose authority?'

'Mine,' Shaw supplied.

Denham's hand was resting on the folder. 'And you want me to look at these results?' he asked Gail.

'Yes, please. I think they're consistent with intermittent porphyria.' The colour of the waste products, neurosis, psychotic behaviour. She had tried to kill herself once – it was on her card. Also she had an addiction for chocolate bars . . . a textbook disease. 'I know it's rare. But it does exist, and if she does have the condition, then the anaesthetic might prove dangerous, could possibly kill her.'

Shaw uncrossed his legs and shifted his position on the chair. 'I've already told Doctor Henderson that I've performed surgery on Mrs Lawson with no ill-effects,' he said to Denham.

'But when, Raymond?' Denham queried sharply. 'When was the last time?'

'Oh . . . ten, possibly eleven years ago.'

'That's a long time.' Denham had still made no move to open Gail's folder.

Gail glanced at Shaw, then quietly addressed Denham. 'I have a great respect for Doctor Shaw's work,' she said, 'and I certainly didn't want him to risk losing a patient on the operating table. Not when it was avoidable.'

'You took your findings to Doctor Shaw?'

'Yes, I . . .' Gail began, but Shaw interrupted her.

'I also told Doctor Henderson what the odds of porphyria were.'

'But as Doctor Henderson says,' Denham mildly pointed out to him, 'it does exist.'

'Look . . .' Shaw's cheeks reddened. 'Am I the one who's on trial here?' he demanded.

'No one's on trial here,' Denham said calmly. He turned back to Gail. 'After you'd had your discussion with Doctor Shaw . . .' he prompted.

'I felt he had to stop the operation. I advised Mrs Lawson to withdraw her permission.

'I see,' Denham said.

'A clear case of unethical conduct,' Shaw stated irritably.

Denham was frowning thoughtfully down at the folder. He looked at Shaw and tapped the folder with his forefinger. 'Do you mind if I take a look at these?'

'I can hardly refuse.' All the same, Gail could see

he wasn't happy about it.

Denham offered him a sop to his offended dignity. 'Naturally, I'd like to have your opinion.'

'I could give you that now,' Shaw said shortly. 'But, by all means, let's take a look.'

Denham looked up at Gail. 'Thank you, Doctor. You may go now.' Gail stood up. 'I'll be in touch again. And, please, in the meantime, do try and remember that there are such things as official channels.'

When the patient's hand came off in her own, Nurse Gordon screamed, and recoiling, knocked both of the kidney bowls, each of them containing a hypodermic needle, off the table where she had placed them only moments before. Hearing the scream and the clatter the bowls made as they fell, Sister Scott came running back into the ward. 'Nurse, what *is* going on here?' she demanded.

Looking stunned, Jill Gordon was still holding the detached hand. The two men in the ward were laughing uproariously. Taking in the scene at a glance, Sister Scott realised what had happened; those two buffoons had just played another of their tasteless tricks on the unsuspecting.

'It's my fault, Sister,' one of them said, still chuckling.

'Back into bed, Mister Bradley,' Sister Scott ordered.

He had just recovered the bowls and syringes from the floor. Putting them down on the table, he climbed back into bed. 'You shouldn't have both of those needles out of the trolley at the same time,' Sister Scott reproached the nurse. 'That's how accidents happen.'

'I'm sorry, Sister,' Jill said meekly. 'It won't happen again.'

Sister Scott looked sourly at the two practical jokers. She'd had just about enough of their stupid tricks – gorilla masks to frighten the nurses, Laurel and Hardy masks – and now a detachable hand. Apparently, they were both commercial travellers who dealt in these sorts of novelties. 'And if you can't behave yourself, Mister Bradley, you'd better find yourself another hospital.'

But while they were still in *this* hospital, they needed their medication. They needed their injections. She picked up the first of the loaded syringes.

Later that morning, when accompanied by Nurse Gordon, she called back into the ward to check on them, she saw that Les Bradley was asleep. The other man, Fred Russell, was sitting up in bed with a pair of headphones, listening to the radio. Grace signalled him to remove them.

'Mister Russell, your doctor says you're ready to be discharged. He wants me to make sure you clearly understand one or two things. Firstly, that your form of diabetes is what is known as "brittle". It's unstable, and you must remember your insulin . . .'

There was a soft moan from the next bed. Les Bradley opened his eyes. 'Sister . . .'

Sister Scott looked at him in disapproval. If this

was another of his tricks . . . He moaned again, and again. Then his eyes opened. 'Sister . . .'

She couldn't take the chance that it wasn't a trick. Moving across to his bed, she examined him briefly. She didn't like what she saw. 'Has he been like this for long?' she asked Fred Russell.

He shrugged. 'I've been listening to the radio,' he said soberly.

Sister Scott looked sharply up at the nurse. 'Get Doctor Steele,' she commanded. 'Emergency paging system. Insulin overdose. Hypoglaecemic attack. Got that?'

The nurse was hurrying out of the room, repeating what Sister Scott had just told her. 'Insulin oh-dee, hypoglaecemic attack . . .'

Within minutes, she was injecting glucose into the arm of the comatose man. 'You're both diabetics,' she explained to Fred Russell. 'You're high dosage insulin, he's low dosage. With all that horseplay this morning, could he have got the wrong needle?'

The needle was in the vein. She released the pressure on the inflatable bandage around the upper part of his arm.

'Yes, he could,' Fred said unhappily.

The plunger was depressed; the glucose was shooting into the vein. Withdrawing the needle, Sister Scott clamped a pad on the vein.

'Later, I'll want to know how.' Then, as Doctor Steele hurried into the room, she said to him, 'I've hit him intravenously with enough glucose to get him out of danger.'

'Thanks, Sister.' Steele looked relieved as he took over his patient.

The glucose drip was attached to Les Bradley's arm, while the man in the next bed watched the proceedings with some apprehension. 'Sister Scott,' Steele said after making certain the attachment was secure, that everything was functioning as it should, 'how does a diabetic patient manage to have a hypoglaecemic attack in a well-run ward?'

Grace Scott had been wondering that herself. 'It's difficult to prove now, but I think he had the wrong insulin dosage earlier in the day.'

Steele regarded her coldly. He was a rather cold man who lived only for his work. Dedicated, was how many people described him. 'And how could that happen? In a well-run ward?'

How indeed? 'I'll take care of that, Doctor,' she said evenly. 'It's a problem of discipline,' she added when she intercepted his bleak look.

'It's a disgrace, that's all I can say,' Steele said, turning on his heel and walking out of the room.

Angry at having been reprimanded in front of a junior, and determined not to have her chain of command interfered with in any way, Sister Scott rounded on the nurse. 'What *did* happen this morning?' she demanded.

Jill Gordon was nervous. She was new – and even though she was Helen's daughter, Grace Scott was showing her no favouritism. 'I helped bring the medication trolley in here for you as you told me,' she said. 'I put the bowl with Mister Russell's needle on his side of the table.' She pointed to the place. 'Then the bowl with Mister Bradley's needle . . . there. And then Mister Bradley put his hand up. He was moaning. I thought he was having an attack . . . It certainly looked that way. At least, I thought it was his hand, but it was a rubber joke hand . . . and it came off . . . and I screamed, and then you came in. You gave them their injections.'

That was right. That was what she had done. 'But if Mister Bradley *did* get the stronger insulin dose meant for Mister Russell,' Sister Scott said thoughtfully, 'and the bowls were right . . . the error must have ben in the pharmacy.'

'No, Sister.' As she swung to face him, Fred Russell explained his unexpected interruption. 'When Les played the joke with the fake hand, the young lass here jumped back. She knocked the bowls over when she did it.'

That was right. Bradley had just been replacing them when she came into the room. She glared at the nurse.

'Maybe they got switched when Les put them back in place,' Russell suggested.

There was no 'maybe' to it. Sister Scott knew with chilling certainty now what had happened. 'All right, Nurse Gordon,' she said crisply. 'The case is closed. But remember this – one medication out at a time.' She nodded towards the unconscious man attached to the glucose drip. 'All that horse-play. He could have died laughing.'

'Last time I saw Abbie she was that high.' Bunny dropped his hand to a foot or so above the floor.

'She and her Dad were heading off to the States to make their fortunes.' He chuckled softly. 'Good comic, Bert – one of the best. Stand up, double acts, work off a dumb showgirl. Big. Six-foot-three, eighteen stone. Good tap dancer.' Edna listened to him with a smile as she tried to imagine such a large man tap dancing. 'I'm serious,' Bunny said. 'Very light on his feet, he was. Made a beautiful pantomime Dame.' He adopted the exaggerated, mincing attitude of the creature in question, making an entrance with one hand positioned against his rump and his voice rising to a grotesque falsetto. 'My name's Gertrude, but *you* can call me Gert, and leave the rude part out. All the subtle material,' he said, his voice dropping back to normal.

Edna laughed. Bunny was always making her laugh – and goodness knew, it was what she needed. 'So you can say she was born in a trunk.' They were talking about Abbie Singleton.

'You can say. Mum was a showgirl.' Bunny raised his hand above his head. 'Legs that long. She was the captain of the chorus line when Bert married her. Three weeks after Abbie was born, she was back hoofing again.' He looked again at the glossy publicity photographs of Abbie Singleton that had just arrived from America. 'Born in a trunk all right. Big name now. Get the customers in.'

It was all arranged. Abbie Singleton was coming. She would perform at Bunny's Place. 'I hope I don't spoil it for you,' Edna remarked quietly.

Bunny looked at her in surprise. 'How could you spoil it for me?'

'Frank,' she said simply. He had written her a letter which she had received the previous morning. It had been a vicious letter. He would get her, he had written, no matter how long it took. He would wait for her. At Bunny's insistence, she had called the police.

'I received some flowers, Mister Bradley.'

'You weren't supposed to know who sent them,' Les Bradley said abashedly.

'Who else would send me a rose called Crimson Passion?' Sister Scott said with just the faintest hint of a smile. 'Really, Mister Bradley, you are transparent.' It was Ada at the kiosk who had told her the rose was called Crimson Passion. Ada had wondered if there was romance in the air; Grace knew she would like nothing better than to have something new to talk about. 'They were very nice, but there was no need.'

'Well, the doctor said I owed you my life.'

'Did he indeed? Which one?'

'The rude one.'

'Doctor Steele's a very busy man.'

'All the same . . .'

'There was no need for the flowers, Mister Bradley,' Sister Scott said. 'I was just doing what I am paid to do.'

'What did the police say?'

‘Frank has already had a mad streak,’ Edna said reflectively. ‘In the eighteen months we were married . . . I guess I knew it even before we were married. But now, Bunny, he’s really gone around the bend.’

‘What happened?’

It was lunch time. There were about half a dozen people in the restaurant. Bunny was behind the bar. ‘They wanted me to look at the film taken during a bank hold-up yesterday. The bandit fired a shot. It turned out the bullet came from the same gun that shot Doctor Rothwell.’

‘So you looked at the film,’ Bunny prompted as he placed a carafe of red wine and two glasses on a tray.

‘It *was* him. He had a stocking over his face, but it was him all right.’

Bunny frowned. ‘Edna, he’s getting desperate. Taking rope. Sooner or later, he’ll hang himself. They’ll catch him – don’t worry.’

‘He’s desperate all right,’ Edna said with certainty. ‘Desperate for money. And Bunny . . .’ she regarded him keenly . . . ‘I keep thinking that if only I’d given him everything from the sale of the farm . . . I don’t need that money so much that innocent people should have to be killed. I should have just given in.’

Bunny took her hand. They were partners now. ‘Look, love, he’d probably still be doing exactly what he’s doing now. And a world where we gave into thugs . . .’ he shook his head dolefully . . . ‘well, that would be no sort of world at all.’

That was all very well for him to say. It did nothing to lessen Edna's heavy feeling of guilt. 'And if I cause someone to die?' she asked shakily. 'Just for some money?' She shook her head. That didn't sound fair to her at all.

It was almost midnight. Edna was polishing the last of the glasses and setting them out on a tray. She was tired; it had been quite a busy day. In a couple of days or so, she thought, it would be even busier; that was when Abbie Singleton would be giving the first of her shows at Bunny's Place, the foyer of which was already decorated with the pictures of her that had been sent from America. Then, hearing the side door close, and thinking that Jim Howard had just returned from the hospital, she called, 'Be sure and bolt that door, Jim.' Bunny had already gone upstairs.

She was just straightening again after placing the tray of glasses on its shelf beneath the counter when, suddenly, a hand clamped over her throat and a voice whispered hoarsely in her ear, 'I warned you, Edna. I warned you that I would get even.'

6

It was so sudden, she had been so totally unprepared . . . and now the terror was back. She could feel her legs giving way beneath her. Warning her not to scream for help, he took his hand from her mouth. He had a gun which, even while he was pouring himself a stiff whisky from behind the bar, he kept pointed at her. Edna was trembling.

'You're looking all right,' he remarked after swallowing almost half the whisky in one gulp. She could see how taut he was, how dangerous. 'Things must be going well for you.'

'You don't need the gun, Frank. I won't call out.'

He drained his glass, then without taking his eyes from her, refilled it from the bottle. With the gun, he gestured to one of the tables. 'Sit down,' he ordered. 'You and I are going to have a little talk.'

Obediently, Edna moved across to the table he had indicated. Frank followed her. They had just sat down when the telephone began to ring. Edna looked at Frank. He shook his head. The telephone continued to ring. Edna heard a sound from upstairs, a bump, a muttered curse, then, drawing his dressing gown around him, Bunny was hurrying down the stairs to still the strident demands of the telephone. 'I'm coming,' he cried impatiently. 'I'm coming.'

Frank had moved around the table to stand behind Edna who was now between him and Bunny. 'Hold it right there,' Frank commanded as Bunny reached the foot of the stairs.

Bunny stopped and peered into the shadows. 'Who's there?' he cried out in alarm.

Frank was pointing the gun directly at his midriff. Edna was slumped helplessly in the chair. Poor Bunny – he shouldn't have been dragged into this. It was all her fault. She should have gone far away, another city, somewhere where Frank couldn't find her. 'Don't touch that phone,' Frank instructed Bunny who was still peering perplexedly into the gloom. 'Now, move over here. Slowly. Make it snappy.' The telephone stopped ringing.

Bunny sat at the table beside Edna who gave him an apologetic glance as he pulled the chair back from the table. His own expression tried to be reassuring – but she could tell he was frightened. Frank sat opposite them. 'Is there anyone else up there?'

Bunny shook his head. Edna said, 'No.'

Frank smiled at them woefully. 'Well, just the three of us. Isn't that too cosy for words?'

Bunny's hands were resting on the table. He raised one of them. 'Look . . .'

Frank jerked the revolver up a fraction so that it was now pointed at Bunny's head. 'You were saying . . ?'

'What is it you want?'

'Money.'

'There's no money,' Edna told him.

'That's right,' Bunny said. Edna noticed that there was a sheen of perspiration on his high forehead. She hoped that the strain of all this wouldn't be too much for him. Jim had told her once that his heart wasn't the best.

'That's nothing to do with you, friend.' Frank was holding the gun steady. 'This is between me and my wife.'

'Frank, I invested it,' Edna said.

'Then *un*invest it.'

'I can't . . .'

'She can't,' Bunny said quickly. 'Edna has invested her money in this place. I was in debt. I was about to sell out, then Edna came along and offered to help out.'

Frank Curtis stared at them. Then, his face twisting in anger, he brought his fist heavily down on the table with a dull thud. Frightened by the thought of what he might do now, Edna said, 'So you see. I don't have any money.'

Bunny began to appeal to Frank's sense of survival. 'You know the police are looking for you, so why don't you cut out now, and we'll just forget you were ever here.'

Frank was staring fixedly at Edna. 'Five thousand,' he said in a low voice. 'Find me that, and I'll keep right out of your life. You'll never see me again.'

Even if she couldn't be sure he would keep his word, Edna wished she did have five thousand dollars to give him. But as it was . . . 'I just don't *have* five thousand, Frank.' She was well aware how carefully he needed to be handled; his nerves were stretched to the utmost.

'There's some money in the till,' Bunny suggested. 'Not much, just a couple of hundred dollars . . .'

Without taking his eyes from Bunny, Frank pushed his chair back and stood up. With the gun he motioned Bunny to his feet. Then he pointed it at Edna. 'Don't try to be a hero. The gun's pointed right at Edna.'

He was a desperate man. Edna knew he was capable of shooting her. She stared in fear at the man who had been her husband for eighteen months. Then the doorbell sounded. Everyone froze. It sounded again. 'It's the door,' Bunny said at last.

'Who is it?'

'No idea.'

Nor had Edna. The side door had been left open for Jim. Unless Frank had locked it behind him as he entered. 'Mister Howard?' a voice called distantly from outside as the bell went again. 'Mister Howard? Are you there?' It was a woman's voice. It had a twang. Edna couldn't think who it could be; it wasn't a voice that was familiar to her.

The bell was ringing repeatedly. 'For God's sake, get it,' Frank muttered angrily. 'Before she wakes up the whole street.'

As Bunny hurried to answer the door, Frank moved quickly behind Edna, and before she realised what he was doing, had his hand clamped around her mouth again, the barrel of the gun against her temple. Bunny opened the door, and then the woman was saying brightly, 'I know, I know, it's past midnight, the witching hour, and this crazy woman's on the doorstep. Hi, I'm Abbie Singleton.'

Oh my God, Edna thought in dismay. Abbie Singleton, from America. A celebrity on the door-step and a madman inside. She was doing all the talking, chirping away. 'I know I've grown.' A small doubt crept into her voice. 'You *are* Bunny Howard, aren't you?' Bunny croaked something. 'The last time you saw me, I think I had two teeth missing at the front.'

Then Bunny was managing to say something. 'I wasn't expecting you for another couple of days.'

The door closed. They were coming inside. 'I feel terrible. I should have called you, I know. It's late. But there were reasons . . .'

And then there they were, materialising from the shadows into the dim light, Bunny looking miserable and the young woman with him now looking uncertainly at the table where Frank Curtis was holding the gun to his wife's head. She stopped. 'What's going on here?'

'As you can see,' Bunny said, 'we've got a bit of a problem here.'

'Well, what do you know.' Abbie Singleton sounded impressed. 'I've walked into the middle of a hold-up.' She took a couple of steps further into the light. 'I don't take to trouble. I stay away from any kind of trouble. It's not my business. Okay, if the guy wants money, I say give him the money. Who wants to be a rich corpse?' She stood there, carrying a bag in one hand and a guitar case in the other, staring at the scene with mild interest.

Frank gestured to Bunny with the gun. 'Back here, where I can keep an eye on you,' he ordered.

With a helpless shrug to Abbie, Bunny moved back to the table. Abbie placed her bag and guitar case on the floor. 'I need a drink,' she said.

Taking his hand from Edna's mouth, Frank Curtis picked up his own drink and finished it. 'You can get me one while you're at it. Scotch.'

'Bourbon for me.' Abbie gave Bunny a questioning look. Bunny nodded. They watched her as she moved behind the bar and took down two glasses.

'Frank,' Edna pleaded, 'please let us go. It's not too late for you to get away from here.'

'Shut up,' Frank growled.

Abbie was pouring the drinks. 'Have you checked the cash register?' she asked Frank.

Frank glanced quickly at Bunny. 'Not yet.'

Abbie put the glasses down on the counter then pressed one of the cash register keys. The 'No Sale' sign came up, and the door slid open. 'Allow me,' Abbie said, peering into the drawer. 'This scene is making me very tired. I want to go to bed. It's been a long day.' She reached into the drawer and taking out a handful of bank notes, riffled through them.

'There's maybe a couple of hundred bucks here,' she announced at last.' She placed the money on the counter beside the cash register and looked inquiringly across at Frank. 'Okay?'

'There's more to it than just the money,' Frank told her. 'It's personal.'

Abbie shrugged. 'I can't believe it,' Bunny said quietly and in a tone of wonder to Edna. 'She was the sweetest little girl, the loveliest kid you could imagine . . .'

Frank rounded on him. 'Will you shut up,' he cried.

'Let them go, Frank,' Edna begged him. 'I'll come with you. I'll do anything you want . . .'

Frank's voice cut sharply across hers. 'Get me five thousand dollars.'

Abbie was coming around the bar with the two drinks. 'You do this for a living, or for kicks?' she asked Frank. She went on, quite conversationally, when he didn't answer, 'You know, for a while I lived with a guy who made his living by mugging people in Central Park. No kidding. I didn't find out right away. I kept finding these wallets. Eventually, the janitor quit because the smell of burning leather was affecting his lungs.' She held out a glass to Frank. 'There you go, Comrade.'

Taking the glass, Frank downed half his drink in one swallow. Abbie watched him closely. Then, as he lowered his glass, she raised her own, tilting it slightly. 'Salud,' she said, the abruptly dashed the contents of her glass into his face.

It all happened so suddenly. Frank yelped as the

liquid splashed into his eyes. Instinctively, he clutched his face, dropping both his glass, which shattered on the floor, and his gun. Abbie made a dive for the gun, which was under the table. She couldn't reach it. 'The gun,' she cried to Edna who just rising to her feet. 'It's on your side.'

Edna reacted quickly. With Frank still crying out in rage and pain, she reached down from the gun which was just by her foot. She scooped it up just as Abbie Singleton aimed a sharp kick at Frank's shin. Shakily, she raised the gun and pointed it at Frank, who, just about to make a lunge at Abbie, was brought up short by the sight of the gun in her hand. Edna glanced at Bunny. 'Call the police,' she ordered. Bunny hesitated, the apparently having assured himself that the situation was under control, moved across the room to the telephone. 'If you make one move, Frank,' Edna said menacingly, 'I'll kill you.' She meant it. She could quite easily have killed him at that moment.

'I'll come straight to the point, Doctor Henderson. I have to say, and I don't particularly like to say it, that I consider your conduct in this matter to have been highly unprofessional.'

Gail Henderson took a deep breath. She had come to the Medical Superintendent's office expecting the worst; now it looked as though her forebodings were justified. 'You were wrong in approaching Mrs Lawson directly, as you did,' Denham went on. 'You have absolutely no right to interfere with another doctor's patient. And in placing yourself in open opposition to him you have embarrassed not only the doctor in question but the hospital as well.' Gail sat stiffly on the chair in front of Denham's desk and stared back at him in defiance. Let him say what he liked, but she still felt she had done the right thing. Denham droned on. 'A hospital must have rules, like any other body or institution. Rules must be observed.'

'I *did* approach Doctor Shaw about my findings,' Gail ventured.

'I'm aware of that,' Denham said. 'I'm also aware that you were correct in your diagnosis.' He allowed himself a thin smile. 'Yes, that's right. We studied those tests you made on Mrs Lawson very carefully. If Doctor Shaw *had* operated, there's no doubt that Mrs Lawson could have been in great danger. She could have even died.'

Gail was staring at him in growing indignation. It was the woman's life which, in any set of circumstances, should have been the main consideration. As for the rest . . . 'And you're telling me I was in the *wrong*?'

Denham pursed his lips. 'I know it's difficult to understand.'

'It's impossible to understand.'

Denham lifted his shoulders in a slight shrug. 'I haven't spoken to Doctor Shaw yet,' he said. 'When I do I'll suggest he owes you an apology.'

'That really isn't necessary.'

'Nevertheless . . .' Denham spread his hands. 'Naturally, I do want you to continue on at the hospital.'

'Will that be all, Doctor Denham?' Gail asked coldly.

Denham nodded. 'I'm sorry you had to go through all this.'

'I'm sorry, too,' Gail said, rising to her feet.

This was becoming ridiculous. So many flowers. Every day a bunch of them. 'You really must stop this, Mister Bradley. It's not that I don't appreciate it . . .'

'A very small gesture, Sister,' Les Bradley said. 'A small thank you to someone who saved my life.'

Sister Scott looked down at the roses she had brought with her into the ward. 'They're really very lovely,' she murmured.

'I'm glad you like them.' Les Bradley was looking quite pleased with himself.

'But every day? It's not necessary – surely. It must be costing you a fortune.'

'That's for me to judge, Sister.'

'Mister Bradley . . .'

'The name's Les.'

'Les, I've got some good news for you. You've been given the all clear. Your pneumonia had completely cleared up. You can leave today, as planned.' Les Bradley's face fell. 'Come on now, you don't have to look so sad. You should be pleased to know that you're fit and healthy again.'

But he didn't look pleased at all.

When Grahame Steele was introduced to Abbie

Singleton on Abbie's opening night at Bunny's Place, the attraction was mutual and immediate. He hadn't intended to go, mainly because he knew there would be a crowd there from the hospital, and he was never one for socialising – but then he had changed his mind. He *was* a fan, after all. He had all her record albums.

The night was a huge success. Abbie sang brilliantly, and the applause was enthusiastic. In the morning, overcoming his customary shyness, Grahame telephoned her at the restaurant. He wondered if it would be possible to come and listen to her rehearsing some of her songs – when and if it would be convenient. Sure, she said. Why not that afternoon, at, say, three o'clock? Grahame hung up with a smile. The prospect of seeing Abbie Singleton again that afternoon made him very happy.

At exactly three o'clock, having arranged with Greg Mason to stand in for him for an hour or so, Grahame presented himself at Bunny's Place where Bunny and Edna Curtis greeted him warmly and told him that Abbie was expecting him. Edna went off to fetch Abbie while Bunny headed for the kitchen to make coffee.

'Hi, there.' Abbie was smiling broadly, quite delightfully at him. It was such a special smile which had held him in its thrall throughout the previous evening. Now it was directed exclusively at him. 'How are you?'

'Looking forward to hearing you rehearse,' Grahame said, his mouth suddenly feeling dry.

'Great. I always appreciate an appreciative audience.'

'That's something you'll always have,' Grahame said gallantly.

Abbie laughed. 'You old flatterer.'

'I really did enjoy last night.'

'Hey, that's good.'

'I'm not one for . . . discos as a rule,' he said ruefully. 'I'm afraid I'm a bit of a square.' He wondered if that was a word still in vogue.

'Really?' Abbie raised her eyebrows. 'You surprise me.'

'But I am. You can ask anyone.' He was well aware what everyone thought of him. He was a square, or whatever it was.

'Then you're a very nice square,' she said.

If such a thing were possible – and Doctor Grahame Steele was a very practical man who had really had no time for such silly fancies or romantic rubbish – he might have said his heart was singing. It certainly felt lighter. He was smiling more than he usually did. 'Don't you go away now,' Abbie said as he moved off to fetch her guitar.

Grahame Steele wasn't going anywhere. Bunny returned with the coffee. 'I hope we'll be seeing more of you, Doctor Steele, he said.

He sat at a table transfixed as Abbie began to sing. 'Will I never learn,' she sang – and she was singing only for him.

Sister Scott's room was beginning to take on the appearance of a florist's shop. Even after he had left the hospital, Les Bradley was still sending flowers to her every day.

'You shouldn't be complaining,' Helen Gordon told her. 'It can't be happening to many girls these days.'

Grace had brought the latest bunch of red roses into Helen Gordon's office. Now she was arranging them in a vase. 'Oh, I'm not complaining. Just spreading the loveliness around a bit.'

'Do you think he's trying to tell you something?'

When she had said goodbye to him at the front steps, Les had asked her if it was possible for them to keep in touch, because that was very much what he wanted to do. She had been embarrassed. No doubt he would forget her the moment he left her, she had remarked. But he had fervently assured her he wouldn't forget her. And, as it turned out, he hadn't. The flowers kept coming.

'He wants to keep in touch, that's all.' She had been sorry to see him go; in a funny way, she missed him.

'He's proving to be a bit of a surprise,' Helen observed. 'I thought all this . . .' she gestured towards the roses which Grace had just finished arranging . . . 'was gratitude, for saving his life. Perhaps he *is* overdoing it a little.'

Grace sighed. 'Anyway,' she said wistfully, 'now that he has gone, I must admit that I did like him. Not at the beginning, though. I didn't like him at all then. All those silly jokes. But after a while . . .' she shook her head . . . 'oh, I don't know. They come and they go, Helen.

Helen Gordon was eyeing her shrewdly from behind her desk. 'You shouldn't be too sure.' she said. 'I have a feeling that Mister Bradley means what he says.'

'Any identification on him?' Greg Mason had the stethoscope to the patient's chest.

'I didn't look,' the orderly replied.

It was another busy day in Casualty. In they came with their broken bones, cuts and bruises. This patient, a man in advanced middle age, had been brought in with a suspected heart attack. As Greg listened for his heartbeat, Jo Jo Adams was checking his pulse. 'Good thinking,' Greg said ironically.

'He collapsed outside the hospital,' the orderly said defensively. 'Near the bus stop. We only had time to rush him here.'

Greg looked up at Jo Jo. 'Pulse?'

'Fast and intermittent.'

Binding the air bag around the upper part of the patient's arm, Greg took his blood pressure. He made a rapid diagnosis. 'His age and general condition . . . mild cyanosis under the eyes . . . pulse rate and blood pressure . . . coronary . . . must be . . .' He turned to the orderly. 'Get him up to Coronary Care.'

As the orderly moved to bring up the trolley, Jo Jo crossed to the telephone. 'Just a moment, please,' Brian Denham said from behind them. Unaware that he had been in the room, they watched him as he walked across to the bed on which the patient was lying. He took the stethoscope from Greg Mason, fitted it, then bending forward, listened first to the patient's lungs, then his heart. After some moments he looked up with an expression of quiet displeasure. 'Have you been through this patient's effects?'

'Not yet, Doctor,' Greg replied.

'Then I suggest that if you do,' Denham said coldly, 'you'll find he carries a card which tell you he's asthmatic. And, if the card won't tell you, I will.'

Greg stared at him in surprise. 'Asthmatic?'

Denham turned to the orderly. 'Take this patient to the Thoracic Ward. My compliments to Doctor Ferguson, and would he treat the case as a matter of urgency.'

'I could have sworn it was a coronary,' Greg said with a baffled shake of his head after the patient had been wheeled away.

'Then, Doctor, you would have been mistaken.'

'But . . . but I examined him.'

'In a most cursory manner,' Denham curtly pointed out to him. 'You saw external systems and were moved to decide that, if it looks like a heart attack, then that's what it is.' He gave Greg a pitying look. 'Diagnosis is partly the science of detection, Doctor. You apparently haven't grasped that fact.'

Greg was stung. 'That's hardly fair, sir . . .'

'Fair?' Denham retorted. 'Would you call sending a patient to the wrong unit, for the wrong treatment, *fair*?' His voice was clipped; he was clearly angry. 'Quite apart from the harm done to your patient, you reveal yourself as clumsy, and my hospital as incompetent. If you *want* to make a fool of yourself, feel free. But not of this hospital – or me. Is that understood?'

'Yes, sir,' Greg said miserably.

There was something wrong with Abbie. She was in a terrible state. Edna had just gone to her room to tell her that Doctor Steele had arrived to pick her up for the day out they had planned to spend together – and there she was, still in bed, in obvious agony, her face deathly pale and shiny with perspiration, a wild and frightened look in her eyes, her breathing fast and shallow. When she saw Edna, she pointed to her bag on the side of the dressing table furthest from the bed. 'My pills,' she gasped. 'Over there . . . in the bag . . .'

Edna was alarmed by her appearance. 'Doctor Steele's downstairs. Should I get him to come up?'

'No!' Abbie exclaimed. 'Just the pills. Please hurry.'

Edna fetched the pills from Abbie's bag. Abbie swallowed them, not bothering to wash them down with water, the flopped back against the pillow. Her breathing was very laboured.

'You need a doctor,' Edna said.

'No, thanks. I've just had one.'

'But you're ill.'

Abbie nodded. She was still having trouble with her breathing. 'Have had . . . better days.'

'But what is it? Can't we help?'

'It . . . it's something I've had for a while.' She gave Edna a faint smile. 'Relax. It looks a lot worse than it is.'

'But you should have a doctor take a look at you.'

'Only if he buys tickets for the show.' Abbie was trying to be her old dry self again. 'You're a sweet lady, Edna,' she took Edna's hand. 'Do you want to do a girl a favour?'

'Of course.'

'The pills . . . they take about an hour to work . . . and I can't see Grahame like this. So . . . be a good cowboy, eh, and cut him off at the pass. Could you do that for me?'

'What will I tell him?'

'Little white lie.' Her breathing was a little easier now. 'Please, Edna.'

'All right then.'

When she told him that Abbie wouldn't be able to keep her date with him, Grahame Steele looked very disappointed. He had been talking to Bunny when Edna came back downstairs. The bunch of flowers he had brought with him lay on the table between them. 'Oh? Is she ill?'

Edna was embarrassed by the need to tell him a lie, but she had promised Abbie. 'No, not ill. She's very tired, that's all. She asked me if you could make it some other time.'

'I see.'

'She really is exhausted,' Edna said emphatically. Too much travel . . . the shows every night. It all catches up.'

Steele's face was set. Edna had the feeling that he

didn't believe her, that he felt he was being given the brush-off. 'I'd like to talk to her.'

Edna knew she wasn't being altogether convincing. 'She . . . sh . . . said she didn't want to be disturbed any more.'

'Disturbed,' Steele said grimly. Edna was only just resisting the urge to tell him the truth. 'I see,' he said again, turning away. 'Good morning.'

They watched him move between the tables to the door. 'What's going on?' Bunny demanded. 'That's the quickest brush-off I've ever seen.'

Edna saw that Doctor Steele had left his flowers behind. She would take them up to Abbie. 'Bunny, she's sick. Really sick.'

'Why didn't you say so? He's a doctor.'

Edna shook her head. 'She won't have a doctor,' she said unhappily. 'She says it will pass. But I don't know *what* to do. When I went to her room just now she, she looked . . . she looked like . . . *death*.'

Grahame Steele was in a foul mood. He was snapping at people more than usual. Back again at his desk in the Casualty ward and buried in a mass of paperwork, he snapped again as someone tapped gently on top of his desk. He didn't look up from the papers spread out in front of him. 'Kindly speak to the duty sister over there. She'll tell you when we want to see you.'

'So is this the famous hot-shot bedside manner?' a familiar voice drawled softly from above his bent head.

Steele looked up sharply. Abbie Singleton was smiling down at him. 'I was told you were exhausted.' He was confused; he had honestly believed that she hadn't wanted to see him.

'So I've come to see the doctor,' she said chirpily. 'This *is* the right place, isn't it.'

'Yes, it is.' The chair beside the desk was stacked high with files. 'Here . . .' Scrambling to his feet, he lifted the files from the chair and placed them on the floor. 'Sit down. Can I get you a coffee, or something?'

Abbie sat down. 'You can take me to the zoo. That was what we originally planned, wasn't it?'

'But, this morning . . .'

'This morning, I woke up with a fit of the meanies,' she said. 'It happens sometimes.'

'Edna told me you were exhausted.'

She waved this away. 'So I put her on the spot. I felt lousy.'

She didn't look tired at all, Grahame Steele decided as he watched her; she looked quite radiant. 'How are you? Really?'

'Fine.' There was a momentary flicker of her eyes. 'Just fine.'

'Abbie, I can't get off now,' Grahame said solemnly. 'I've already upset the schedule once.'

'How about tonight?'

'I don't finish until ten.'

'Fine. I'll book us into a motel.'

'You'll *what*?'

'A motel,' Abbie replied equably. 'They do a beautiful after-ten supper, I'm told. Served in the room . . .'

Grahame stared at her. He had never heard her like this before. So direct . . . 'I'm not entirely sure I understand . . .'

'Yes, I *am* propositioning you,' Abbie said softly, and there was a light in her eyes, a warmth that only added to his confusion. 'There's no show tonight, or tomorrow.' Her smile deepened. How beautiful she was, Grahame Steele thought. 'I'll make all the arrangements. All *you* have to do is decide if you want to come.'

Grahame Steele had already decided. It was what he wanted – very much.

7

The patient was Chinese and couldn't speak English. He had been badly beaten, and he was semi-conscious. He was moaning in agony. Reception had called to say he had just been dumped from a moving car outside the hospital entrance. The Casualty ward was having one of its usual busy Saturday nights.

'Do you think he's been mugged?' Jo Jo Adams queried.

Greg Mason was gently palpating the man's upper abdomen. The patient yelped as Greg struck a tender spot. 'I'd say so.' Greg ran his finger lightly around the outline of one of the many bruises that covered the man's body. 'Someone's given him a devil of a kicking.' He addressed the patient. 'Hold on there, sport. This might hurt a little.'

'He can't understand you,' Jo Jo reminded him.

'Then he'll find out, won't he?' Carefully he began to palpate the man's flesh again. There was another cry of pain. The patient began to struggle. Moving quickly around to the head of the bed, Jo Jo held him down by the shoulders while Greg continued his examination. 'Spleen's enlarged,' he observed. 'Probably ruptured.'

'Do you want me to get him down to X-ray?'

'Hold on. I'll give him a shot for the pain first.'

When the patient saw the needle in Greg's hand, his eyes widened in terror. He began to scream, to struggle again. 'It won't hurt you,' Greg reassured him. 'You won't feel a thing.' Okay, so the man was frightened of needles. So many people were, but they didn't make such a racket about it. This man was obviously terrified, but that couldn't be helped. He needed a shot to deaden the pain. He nodded to Jo Jo to keep holding the patient down, then, deftly, he pushed the needle into the patient's arm where the nurse had just dabbed it with a wad of cotton wool.

For a moment after the needle had penetrated his skin, the patient was perfectly relaxed. Then, suddenly, the patient's body arched wildly up from the bed as if it had just received a massive electric shock, before collapsing again. Greg swore. The patient was lying very still, the terror still stamped in his now unseeing eyes.

'Oxygen!' Greg yelled to Jo Jo who was on her way to the telephone. She came running back.

'What happened?'

'*Move!*'

Frantically, he was feeling for the carotid pulse. There was none. He began to hammer the man's chest with his fists in an attempt to start the heart moving again as Jo Jo slipped the oxygen mask over the man's face.

'Pulse.'

Jo Jo felt for the pulse, then looking up, shook

her head. 'Nothing.'

Greg swore again. He was still pummelling the patient's chest. 'Fibrillator.'

He didn't stop his pounding. 'Don't die,' he muttered savagely. 'Don't you *dare* die on me.' He grabbed the fibrillator from Jo Jo when she brought it to him, and placed the terminals against the man's chest. 'Zap him,' he ordered.

Jo Jo turned the knob on the machine. As the current hit, the man's body arched again then flopped lifelessly back onto the bed. There was still no pulse. 'Again.'

'But, Doctor . . .'

'You heard me.'

Again, the body was jolted by the electric current. Again it dropped loosely back onto the bed. And again, there was no pulse. 'Adrenalin.'

'Adrenalin?'

'For God's sake, Nurse . . .'

But neither was there any response from the adrenalin. In anger and frustration, Greg tossed the empty syringe into a tray. There was nothing else he could do for the man now; he had tried everything. He stared down at the patient. He didn't bother to touch him. He didn't need Jo Jo to tell him, after she had checked the man's pulse for one last time, that he was dead. Worse than that, he knew that he had killed him.

'All right, Doctor. We'll take it from the top, shall we?'

'It was anaphylactic shock.'

'So you're now performing post mortems by remote control,' Brian Denham said coldly, 'as well as diagnosis.'

The police had come and gone. They would know nothing for certain about the man's death until after the post mortem. Greg Mason had already been giving it a lot of thought.

'He *knew* it was going to happen,' Greg said. 'I swear it. As soon as he saw the needle . . .'

The were in Denham's office. Denham was eyeing him with hostility. 'Are you, Doctor, among your many other remarkable talents, fluent in Chinese?'

'Of course not.'

'Of course.' Denham nodded as if something had just been confirmed to him. He glanced up at Jo Jo Adams who was standing by the wall. 'And it's rare for a patient to be prescient about his own death from anaphylactic shock – if, indeed, that's what killed him. I mean, he could hardly have had previous experience . . .' he smiled unpleasantly . . .' could he, Doctor?'

'No, sir,' Greg muttered.

'No, sir,' Denham echoed. 'Right.' He leaned forward over his chair, his eyes boring into Greg's like gimlets. 'Now, if you'll be so kind, detail for me exactly, while it's still as clear as it ever will be in your mind, the symptoms and your interpretation of them.'

Greg shifted in his chair. This examination wasn't making him feel any better about what had happened, as necessary as he realised it was. Mentally, he shuffled the sequence of events into their proper order. 'The patient was brought in after being thrown from a moving car. He couldn't speak English, but was obviously in great pain. An examination revealed a distended spleen, extensive bruising, and possible internal injury . . . .'

'Did you consider sending the patient to X-ray,' Brian Denham interrupted him.

Denham knew very well that the patient hadn't been sent to X-ray. 'I was going to do that after giving him a morphine injection for the pain,' he said uncomfortably.

'Having first tested for any possible allergies to morphine, of course.'

Greg didn't like the other man's sarcasm. 'There wasn't time,' he protested. 'The man was in intense pain. I didn't know the full extent of the injuries. He was obviously in pain.'

'Well, he sure as hell isn't in pain now.' Denham brought the flat of his hand down on the desk. 'So, if you don't mind, Doctor, we'll wait until the results of the autopsy before determining *how* the patient died, and then we'll look – very closely, I might add – at *why* he died.'

They not only had dinner in the motel room, but breakfast as well. Abbie placed the teapot and a quartered orange in front of Grahame, kissed him lightly on the top of his head and said something about tea and oranges coming all the way from China. 'Eat your oranges,' she urged him. 'Keep your strength up.'

'I won't be doing anything strenuous.'

She gave him a sly look. 'That's what *you* think.'

Grahame Steele was a man hopelessly in love. The night they had just spent, between supper and breakfast, had been the most perfect, the most *total*, experience of his life. He reached for her hand. 'I love you, Abbie Singleton.' She stared down at him. 'It's true.'

If she had been wistful for that brief moment, she quickly shook it off. 'You'll have me bawling in my bacon next.' She snapped her fingers. 'Hey, there's a great song . . . Bawlin' in the Bacon – have you heard it?'

'Everything's a joke to you, isn't it?' Grahame said with a shake of his head.

Her smile disappeared. 'Not everything, Hotshot,' she said a little sadly, then immediately brightened again. 'Hey, come on, eat your breakfast. You don't want it to get cold.'

They ate their breakfast. They talked, lightly, jokingly – and then, when Grahame glanced at his watch and saw what time it was, he jumped to his feet in consternation. He hadn't realised it was so late.

'What's wrong?'

He reached for his jacket. 'I'm on duty. I'll be late. I've never been late before.'

'What about me?' She was looking up at him with a concerned expression. 'You can't just leave me here like this.'

He shrugged himself into his jacket. 'I'll see you at Bunny's. As soon as I come off duty.'

'*No!*' she was on her feet, facing him. Grahame was startled by the desperation in her voice, in her eyes.

'But I can't just not turn up.'

'Call them. Make some excuse.' She was clutching his sleeve.

'Abbie, you don't understand . . .'

'No, *you* don't understand. This is *our* time, Grahame. Your time and mine.'

'There'll be other times. Many more times.'

Grahame couldn't understand why she should be so upset. She was almost panicking. 'You don't *know* that.' Her fingers dug into his arm. 'Please, darling,' she implored, now with tears in her eyes. 'Don't leave me.'

8

It was Edna Curtis who found her, slumped in a chair in her room, her eyes wide and staring as she struggled for breath. She looked ghastly. She looked even worse than she had when Edna had found her still in bed that morning when Grahame Steele had arrived with a bunch of flowers to take her out for the first time.

And again, it was because Grahame Steele was trying to reach her that she had come up to her room, to find her in such a wretched condition.

'Abbie?' She hurried into the room. Abbie raised her head. Her eyes were filmy. 'Edna . . . please . . . help me.' Her head dropped again.

Grahame had called because Abbie hadn't turned up for their date. It had been an hour or more since her evening's performance had ended – and, as usual, it had been a huge success – and Grahame had been worried about her. Edna knew it wasn't like Abbie; she knew how close the two of them had become over the past few weeks, always going out somewhere, doing things together . . . It was perfectly plain to everyone how much in love the two of them were. Edna hurried downstairs where she hoped she would still find Doctor Raymond Shaw who had come in to watch the show, and afterwards, had stayed on to have a few drinks with Bunny. She was in luck.

'And she was unconscious when you came in?' Shaw asked Edna after he and Bunny had laid Abbie on the bed.

'Not quite. She asked for help. She recognised me.'

Taking his keys from his pocket, Shaw handed them to Bunny. 'My bag's in the car. Out front.' Bunny nodded and hurried away. Shaw took Abbie's pulse. He frowned, then raising her eyelids, peered into her eyes. 'Do you know if she was taking any medication?'

'Medication?' Edna tried to think. 'There were her pills, of course.'

Shaw looked sharply at her. 'What pills?'

'Oh, I don't know what they were for . . .' She had the impression that Shaw already knew what they were for. 'I always thought they were some form of vitamins, the way she was taking them all the time . . .'

'Where did she keep them?'

'I don't know. Perhaps in her bag . . .'

Seeing Abbie's bag on the dressing table, Shaw picked it up, and opening it, took out a bottle. 'These ones? These pills?'

The bottle looked familiar. Edna nodded. 'That's them.' She could hear Bunny's footsteps on the stairs outside the room.

Shaw was frowning again as he studied the label on the bottle. Bunny came into the room with Shaw's bag. Shaw took it from him, and opening it, found his stethoscope. 'Get an ambulance,' he instructed Bunny.

'Right.' Bunny was already moving back to the door.

'And call Sister Scott. Have her notify Intensive Care, then ask her to find Doctor Harvey, have him come over to the hospital at once. On my authority. Have you got that?'

'Harvey,' Bunny muttered as he left the room. 'Got it.'

On the bed, Abbie was breathing raggedly. Shaw stared sadly down at her. 'The poor kid,' he murmured.

It was a long wait at the hospital. Bunny was pacing up and down the length of the visitors' waiting area. 'You'd think they'd tell us *something*,' he complained. 'What's wrong with her. Where she is . . .'

'She's in Intensive Care,' Edna told him. 'Upstairs.'

Bunny wheeled towards the lifts. 'Well, I'm going up there. Get some sense out of someone.'

Catching up with him, Edna grasped his arm. 'No, Bunny, please. Don't make a scene.'

'I'm *not* making a scene,' Bunny said heatedly. 'I just want to know. I have a *right* to know, haven't I? I mean, *I'm* the one who's responsible for her.' He slammed his fist into the palm of his other hand. His face was flushed. 'What am I going to tell her Dad . . ?' He broke off as something occurred to him. 'Of course,' he said, more quietly. 'I can't tell him anything.' He stared bleakly at Edna. 'He's on the road, isn't he? Playing some whistle-stop somewhere in the middle of America. I don't even know where to call him.'

'Perhaps Abbie will know . . .'

'She can't tell us, can she?'

'I don't know . . .'

Bunny began to pace again. 'You think her agent would have known if she was sick. Before she came out here . . .' He stopped his pacing, then swung back to face Edna. 'Hey, there's a thought. Abbie has the same agent as her Dad. *That's* how I'll find him.'

The lift doors opened, and Jim Howard stepped out into the waiting area. Edna studied his face for a sign of hope, but saw none. Bunny moved quickly across to his son. 'About time, too,' he said tersely. 'We were nearly going out of our heads.'

Edna was more concerned with coming to the point. 'How is she, Jim?'

Jim shook his head solemnly. 'Not good,' he said. 'She's in Intensive Care. It's not good at all.'

'What's the matter with her?' Bunny asked in a subdued voice.

Jim looked at them both. 'It's a chronic condition, and in most cases . . . it's terminal.'

They stared at him. Bunny was the first to speak. 'You mean, she's going to die?'

'We're doing everything we possibly can, Dad.'

Impatiently, Bunny waved this aside. 'Is she going to recover – or isn't she?'

But there was still nothing in Jim Howard's expression that offered even the faintest hope.

'He's won, hasn't he? He's drawn the winning card.'

'Who's that?'

'The old man with the scythe.' Abbie raised her hand a little from the sheet. 'Zot! Got me!'

'You're doing fine,' Shaw said thickly.

'You're a sweet liar.'

He had just given her a shot to ease the pain. 'We've taken tests, and . . .'

'They took all the tests.' Abbie gestured again, weakly. 'Six months ago, at John Hopkins. Good hospital. Know their stuff. Gave me a bottle of pills. "Go away and die." Only honest answer, isn't it, Doc?'

'There are new discoveries. New advances are being made every day.' He knew it was hopeless to try and reassure her. She knew she was going to die.

'Can't wait that long. Wish I could . . .'

'You should rest.'

'Soon.' The pale, drained woman in the bed managed the shadow of a smile. 'I'll have all the rest I need. On and on . . . nothing but rest.' Her eyes clouded. 'Who . . . who's going to look after Dad now? Getting old. And Hotshot. Poor old Hotshot . . .' Her eyes closed. With an alarmed glance up at Sister Scott who was standing on the other side of the bed, Shaw bent over the dying woman. Her eyes flickered open, and there was that shadowy smile again. 'Still here. Fooled you.'

'We're trying to find Grahame . . .'

'No, please . . .' She moved her head on the

pillow. 'It can't do any good. I want him to remember . . . what it was. You tell him . . . remember the ever-constant now . . . you tell him that . . .'

9

'Well? What happened?'

'What do you mean? What happened?'

'You know very well. Les Bradley.'

'Oh yes, Les Bradley.' Grace Scott smiled archly. 'That's right. I had dinner with him last night, didn't I?'

Helen gave her an exasperated look. It was morning tea time in the Medical Superintendent's outer office. Grace had brought the buns as usual. 'Grace Scott! Are you going to tell me, or not?'

'I had a marvellous time,' Grace told her. 'He didn't put on a gorilla mask and frighten the waiter. He dances well – suspiciously well. He was probably one of those awful young men with slicked-down hair and you-know-what on their minds, who haunted the Saturday night dances.'

'He must have changed since then,' Helen remarked.

'Oh, he was the perfect gentleman.' Grace became more serious. 'I hope he doesn't try anything, Helen. I just don't think I could stand it if he did.'

Helen laughed as she refilled Grace's cup from the teapot. 'Come on now. Don't let's start worrying about that sort of thing.'

'It's life.' Grace was still serious. 'It's going to come to that.'

Helen raised her eyebrows. 'How do you know that? Why can't you have a nice platonic friendship?'

'Would a man settle for that, I wonder?'

'Grace,' Helen said deliberately, 'when you meet the right man, you won't want him to settle for anything like that. But, if you *don't* get out with men like Les Bradley, then you'll never find the right person. I don't want to see you end up an old maid. That just shouldn't happen to you.'

Grace Scott sipped her tea. 'He's asked me out again.'

'That's good,' Helen Gordon said with a satisfied nod. 'That's very good. I'm very pleased to hear it.

But Grace Scott still wasn't sure if it *was* such a good thing.

As they sat in their alcove in Bunny's Place, Grace Scott sensed that the time had now come for something as yet nebulous but nevertheless important to be broached. They had finished their dinner, and the mood was perfectly relaxed. Grace felt quite mellow. But there was still that something that needed to be confronted. It had hovered over them all evening.

'Grace, you do like being with me, don't you?' Les was leaning forward across the table. Music was playing softly, unobtrusively. Grace drank some of her wine to cover the sudden nervousness which had been ignited by his own. 'I mean, I don't bore you, or anything like that, do I?'

'I wouldn't be here if you did,' she pointed out to him.

The waiter arrived with a bottle of champagne. Les looked relieved. 'Ah, just what the doctor ordered.'

Grace began to protest. she hadn't realised he had ordered champagne. 'Les . . .'

'Now, Grace.' Les nodded to the waiter who began to pour the champagne. 'There *is* a reason.'

Grace already suspected what the reason was. Perhaps that hovering quality in the air hadn't been so nebulous after all. 'You should always have candlelight,' Les said after the waiter had gone.

Grace laughed self-consciously. 'During the day as well?'

'Well . . .' Les also laughed self-consciously, then became serious again. 'I've been looking at a flat, quite close to the hospital. It's not a bad area to live . . .' He smiled uncertainly, then as his eyes met Grace's across the table in the soft glow of the candlelight, he finally blurted it out. 'Grace,' he said softly, 'Would you marry me?'

So it had come at last. It was out in the open at last, revealed for what it was. Grace sighed. 'I *am* rather set in my ways, Les . . .'

'I know. So am I.'

'I wouldn't be easy to live with . . .'

'I know.' Les was watching her eagerly across the table.'

'But . . .' It was funny, but true. 'I *am* happy when I'm with you.'

'I know.'

'It's a big step.'

'I know, Grace.'

'We're both used to living alone,' she said.

'So we could get used to living together,' he put in quickly.

'But I would like to think about it.'

'Then will you come and look at the flat?'

'Yes.'

'Tomorrow?'

'Tomorrow's fine,' she said. 'I'm off duty in the afternoon.' She smiled. 'Thank you, Les.'

Les raised his glass of champagne. Grace raised her own glass. They toasted each other in silence.

Philip Winter was a celebrity. He was also very rich which was why Raymond Shaw was insistent he should have everything he needed during his stay in the hospital as Shaw's private patient. As Chairman of the Hospital Board, he was particularly desirous of obtaining a substantial donation for his pet project, a new Children's wing. He wanted Winter to be handled with kid gloves. Sister Scott wasn't impressed; as far as she was concerned, *all* patients were VIPs. Already, the private ward that had been allocated to the great man was full of flowers and telegrams from a legion of female admirers; he was also a very good looking man.

Hilary Templeton seemed quite satisfied with the arrangements. The only thing that didn't please her was the nurse that had been assigned to her employer. 'She really is most unsuitable,' she said after the nurse had been dismissed.

Sister Scott's expression during this tour of inspection had remained completely impassive. 'Nurse Warner is young,' she said flatly, 'but has had Private Nursing experience. She's highly qualified.'

Hilary Templeton was Philip Winter's private secretary. Immaculately groomed, she was blonde and rather pouting. Her manner throughout had been brusque. 'I'm sure she is, Sister,' she said with a sweetness edged with steel. 'But Mister Winter has an image you see, of always being surrounded by young women. Would you have someone on the staff who is a little more . . . photogenic?'

She had already told them that Winter would be accompanied by photographers on his arrival. She had told Shaw that she would like him and a nurse to pose with him. Then she had asked to see the nurse that had been assigned to him. Julie Warner might have been capable, but she was really rather plain – Shaw conceded that. She wore glasses. Hardly the image. 'I'll look after this, Sister Scott,' he said hurriedly as he noticed the stiffness of her reaction. 'Of course, I understand perfectly, Miss Templeton,' he said after Sister Scott had left the room. 'I'm sure we can come up with someone suitable for your needs.'

Raymond Shaw was very put out. They had been expecting their VIP to arrive that afternoon. He had been waiting for a half an hour in the reception area for him to arrive – and now here was this Hilary Templeton telling him, as cool as you please, that unfortunately Winter wouldn't be able to make it today after all. She'd had a telephone call from him. He had asked her to pass on his regrets. She was sorry, too.

'And so am I,' Shaw said testily. 'Does he realise that I've re-scheduled my entire day to suit him? And it *has* been very difficult to organise things. I hope he's aware of the inconvenience this is causing a number of people.'

'And, as I've told you, Doctor Shaw,' she said coolly, 'he apologises. The circumstances were entirely beyond his control.' She paused and regarded him levelly with her large green eyes. 'Anyway, I should point out that Mister Winter is paying a great deal of money for his private room here. *And* for your personal services as his surgeon.'

'I'm aware of that fact,' Shaw muttered.

Hilary Templeton was pressing the point home. 'There *are* other hospitals, Doctor Shaw, if you're not happy with the situation. If you *would* prefer to terminate the arrangements we've made, I'm sure I would have no trouble booking Mister Winter in elsewhere.'

What an appalling woman, Shaw thought. 'Perhaps you should discuss the possibility with Mister Winter,' he suggested.

She shook her head. 'There's no need for me to bother Mister Winter.' She gave him one of her sweetly-laced smiles. 'I'll leave it to you, Doctor, to contact me if you prefer to cancel the arrangement. We'll be most hapy to oblige.'

'Very well then,' Shaw said decisively. 'I'll cancel the booking.'

'Damn me, Brian, that woman is the most irritating female I've ever met. A beautiful iceberg. How Winter puts up with her I'll never know.'

'She's probably very efficient,' Brian Denham suggested.

Shaw had no doubt about that. 'There'd be no other attraction,' he said. 'Anyway, the room's available. After all the fuss and bother we can let another patient have it . . .' He smiled ruefully. 'Flowers and all.'

'The Winter of our discontent,' Denham mused.

'OH, very good, very droll.' Shaw sighed. 'God, how I did want that two hundred thousand from him for the new wing.'

Helen Gordon came into the office with some files which she placed on Denham's desk. Denham looked up at her. 'Helen, please advise the department they can use the private room we had booked for Philip Winter.'

'What happened?'

'Hilary Templeton,' Shaw said in disgust. 'That's what happened.'

'I'll tell the department.' Helen Gordon left the room.

'You know, I could *feel* that cheque in my pocket,' Shaw wailed.

'So maybe we'll find another Santa Claus.' Denham didn't seem to be too put out by this disappointing turn in their fortunes. Shaw glared at him resentfully.

'Santa Clauses, like Philip Winters, are very few and far between and they're becoming scarcer.'

'I wonder what it's like to be a guy like Winter,' Denham mused.

'Very comfortable.'

'All that power . . . generated by money. Manipulating people . . . companies . . . playing chess on a map of the world.'

'Let's not forget the ladies,' Shaw said enviously. 'Beautiful ladies.'

'It must be a busy life,' Denham said with a smile.

'*Damn* that Templeton woman.' Shaw brought his hand down on the desk. If it hadn't been for her . . . . Helen Gordon came back into the office.

'Miss Templeton is outside,' she told Denham. 'She would like to speak to you and Doctor Shaw.'

'Show her in, Helen,' Denham said while Shaw wondered if the Templeton woman had heard his outburst.

They stood up as Hilary Templeton entered the office. Shaw noted that she wasn't looking quite so assured as she had done earlier. 'I have just spoken to my employer,' she said after Denham had introduced himself and invited her to sit down. 'He has instructed me to apologise to you, Doctor Shaw, and to tell you that the arrangements stand.' Shaw exchanged a quick, triumphant glance with

Denham. He hoped Winter had given his private secretary a proper bawling-out. 'He refuses to allow any other surgeon in Australia to operate on his knee.'

Now, that was more like it. That was what Shaw wanted to hear. He assumed a look of ferocious modesty. 'Well, now . . .'

Hilary Templeton was looking at him with just a trace of contrition. 'I hope you'll forgive me for our misunderstanding earlier – and I also hope you'll reconsider taking Mister Winter as your patient.'

It must have been a torrid session, Shaw thought with satisfaction – short and sharp, and very much to the point. 'Well, Miss Templeton . . . I accept your apology, and, yes, I'll be more than happy to attend to Mister Winter.' He was being thoroughly gracious about this; he was in command again. 'May we know when we are to be honoured by his presence? To save causing a great deal of inconvenience all round.'

'Yes, of course.' Shaw knew she wasn't enjoying the need to eat humble pie. 'Mister Winter said he could come today – if you wish.'

'Ah . . .' Shaw shook his head regretfully. 'I'm afraid it's not longer convenient for him to arrive today.' He was enjoying this. He pretended to consider. 'I may be able to fit him in some time next week. If you could phone my secretary tomorrow I'm sure she'll find a time that's mutually suitable.'

Hilary Templeton's smile was pained and fleeting. '*Touché.*' She stood up. 'I'll tell Mister Winter.'

Denham and Shaw were also standing. 'I'll see that the flowers are watered every day,' Shaw told her.

Hilary Templeton smiled vaguely. 'By the way, if it's any added incentive to you, Doctor Shaw, I'll be most happy to try and persuade Mister Winter to make a sizeable donation for the new Children's wing.' Now her smile was one of devastating sweetness. 'That's what you're after, isn't it?'

The barb struck home. 'My God!' Shaw exclaimed after she had gone. He rounded on Denham. 'Brian, I'll need that room for Monday. Can you arrange it?'

Denham smiled and shrugged. He seemed to be rather bemused by it all.

The Great Man had arrived for his operation which Raymond Shaw had privately vowed would leave him with the prettiest and most expensive kneecap in the State. Favouring his injured knee and supporting himself on the shoulder of a very attractive young woman, he walked slowly in through the main entrance of the hospital to be greeted by a small reception committee, which included a dark, glamorous creature who Hilary Templeton had introduced to Raymond Shaw, rather icily, as Carolyn Fielding. Shaw had been charmed by her; he had given her one of his courtly, old-fashioned bows.

As Philip Winter came into the reception area, he grinned and waved with his free hand. There was a sudden flash as a photographer, who had ducked around in front of him, took his picture. He came up to the group waiting for him, and took his hand from his escort's shoulder. The photographer took more pictures as he kissed the woman who had been introduced as Carolyn Fielding. 'Hello, Tiger.' Still beaming, he turned to Hilary Templeton. 'Hello, Hilary. Come to bury Caesar, have you?'

'Hardly, Philip,' Hilary said drily.

Winter shook hands with Raymond Shaw. 'Got your knives sharpened?' he asked.

Shaw laughed politely. 'We're certainly ready for you. So is your room.'

Winter gestured to the girl who had brought him. 'Make sure she gets a car back,' he said to Hilary Templeton. 'Fifty bucks.' He glanced at the photographer. 'Go for your life, son.' The photographer took a shot of him shaking hands with Shaw, who blinked in the sudden glare of the flashlight. Winter dropped his hand then placed his arm around Carolyn Fielding's waist. 'Let's check out that room, Tiger. I want your opinion on the bed.'

'Oh, Philip,' the girl chided him gently. 'Don't say things like that.'

Shaw led the way to the private room that had been set aside for Winter who was now using Carolyn Fielding as a prop. 'I missed you, Tiger,' he said.

'I missed you, too.'

They were obviously very close, Shaw thought with the smallest of grimaces. He wondered for how long; Philip Winter, millionaire playboy was not the type to keep his women, of whom there was undoubtedly a limitless supply, for very long. He shoved them into the room where Sister Scott was already waiting for them. 'Very nice,' Winter said as he gazed approvingly around the flower-bedecked room.

Shaw introduced him to Sister Scott. 'Will you be nursing me?' he asked after a quick appraisal of her.

'No, I won't. But, of course, I'll be available if there are any special problems.'

'Then I'll have to see if I can arrange some,' he said as Carolyn Fielding helped him across to the bed. He lowered himself onto it. 'But as long as there's a pretty nurse around, I'll be happy.' A picture was taken of him sitting between Carolyn and Hilary on the bed. 'Where is she, by the way?'

'She should be back any moment,' Sister Scott informed him.

'Good. I'd like to get acquainted.'

Nurse Warner appeared in the doorway. Everyone looked at her. Sister Scott introduced her to Philip Winter who was suddenly not looking so pleased. The photographer readied himself to take a picture of Winter and the nurse. Winter stopped him. 'They've got to be kidding,' he said quietly to Hilary. 'I told you that the nurses have to be attractive. This one . . .' He gestured to the nurse who was clearly not attractive.

Sister Scott caught Shaw's eye. Her expression was grim. Nurse Warner, her face flushed, embarrassed by Winter's rejection of her, was backing away in confusion. 'Doctor Shaw, could I have a word with you? Outside?'

'Of course, Sister.' He smiled at Winter. 'If you'll excuse me. I know you want to get settled in. I'll come back in a little while. We can talk then.'

Out in the corridor, Sister Scott laid down the law. 'Doctor Shaw, I am *not* going to stand idly by and let my staff be insulted by that over-sexed, egocentric . . . *tennis player*.' She kept her voice low. Her words were clipped. She was very angry.

'I'm sorry about that, Sister,' Shaw was now finding himself in something of a dilemma; his patient had to be kept happy at all costs; Sister Scott, too, needed to be placated.

'Don't apologise to me, Doctor. Apologise to Nurse Warner. She's been deeply embarrassed.'

'I know,' Shaw said uncomfortably.

Sister Scott's eyes were like chips of ice as she continued to bore in on him. 'What does he think he's looking for? A nurse or a one-night stand?'

'It's a question of publicity, really,' Shaw said quickly as a way out of the problem presented itself. 'I should have mentioned it. All they want is a pretty nurse to pose with him for some pictures.' Sister Scott made a sound of disgust. Shaw continued to try and make her see reason. 'We can hardly complain, considering that he *may* be making a large donation for our new wing.' He gave her one of his more reassuring smiles. 'Now all we have to do is find a pretty young nurse to pose for a few pictures, then Julie can carry on nursing the man.'

'If you say so, Doctor.' Nurse Scott still didn't look convinced.

'Is there anyone you can suggest?' he asked hopefully.

Sister Scott shook her head. 'I can't imagine,' she said tersely, turning away. 'And I really have more important things to do than participate in this carnival.'

It was Jo Jo Adams's day off, but they were trying to find her after Raymond Shaw had stressed its importance. Jo Jo, he was sure, would suit the bill just nicely.

'We haven't got so much time for this,' Hilary Templeton said impatiently. 'The photographer has a deadline.' Shaw knew that; this insufferable woman had been drumming that into him for the past hour or more. 'And, frankly, I haven't seen any other nurses here so far who *would* be suitable.'

'But you haven't seen all of them,' Shaw protested weakly.

She regarded him coolly. 'I've created a specific image for Philip,' she said. 'That image requires him to be surrounded at all times by beautiful young woman. It's what the public expects.'

'Believe me.' Shaw raised his hands in a gesture of resignation. 'I understand.'

'Now, at times,' Hilary continued, 'he may take this image of his a little seriously.'

'I hope it doesn't cause too many problems,' Shaw remarked.

'It won't, if you don't let it.'

Shaw sighed; this was the last thing with which he wanted to be involved; he was a top surgeon, with wide-reaching responsibilities, not a talent scout. 'You have to understand, Miss Templeton,' he said, 'that while I wish to help all I can, we still have an entire hospital to run.'

Hilary Templeton glanced at her watch. It was just after nine-thirty in the morning. 'Just a few pictures – in exchange for a very large donation.' She looked at him shrewdly. 'A bargain, don't you think?'

A cleft stick was more like it, Shaw thought unhappily. This business was becoming too ridiculous for words. Sister Scott had been right to describe it as a carnival.

'You wanted to see me, Doctor Shaw?'

With a sigh of relief, Shaw turned as Jo Jo Adams walked into the staff room. Surely, he thought, there could be no complaints about *her*. He glanced at Hilary Templeton who gave an approving nod, then walked out of the room. 'Sit down, Jo Jo,' Shaw invited.

In her street clothes, she looked even more seductive. 'I do have a lunch date, Doctor,' she told him.

'This won't take long.' Shaw sat down opposite her. He could see that she was puzzled by this urgent summons. 'It's about Philip Winter.'

'Yes?'

'His business manager has arranged a photographic sesssion for today. For publicity purposes.

She wants some pictures of him taken with his nurse.'

'That's Julie Warner.'

'She doesn't want Julie – for the pictures, that is. They want a young, pretty girl.' It didn't make him happy to say it; Jo Jo was Julie's room mate. 'In short, they want you.'

'I see,' Jo Jo said quietly.

'You'd be doing the hospital a great favour,' Shaw insisted. 'And me.'

'I don't think I can help you, Doctor Shaw.' Jo Jo rose to her feet. 'Today is my day off, and besides, with my busy work schedule for the rest of the week, I don't think I can spare the time.'

'But this is important, Jo Jo.' Shaw was also on his feet.

'I'm sorry, Doctor.'

'Jo Jo, wait.' He hurried after her as she walked quickly out of the room.

He had just reached the doorway when he had to step aside to allow two nurses to pass him as they came into the room. One of them was Julie Warner, but it was the other one who immediately riveted his attention. He had never seen her before; she must have been new to the hospital, he decided. But more than that, she was absolutely stunning. His breath caught in his throat. Ravishing, sultry . . . Jo Jo Adams was immediately forgotten. He watched her as she and Julie Warner settled themselves at one of the tables.

'Excuse me, Doctor Shaw.'

As Sister Scott was about to enter the room behind the two nurses, Shaw impulsively took hold of her arm. 'Who is that?' he asked in low voice, nodding towards the table where the two nurses were sitting and conversing quietly. 'The one with Nurse Warner.' The one with those soulful brown eyes and the sensuous lips, with the . . .

'He name is Kelly Jones,' Sister Scott told him with an air of forebearance.

'New?'

'Yes, but with a lot of experience as a private nurse.'

Better still. Things were beginning to look up. The heavens were opening, truly and marvellously. 'Well, well, well,' he murmured. 'I would say that that's just perfect. Sister Scott.' He was still holding her arm.

'Yes?' She eyed him dubiously.

'Sister Scott, I would like you to do me a very great favour,' he said.

Kelly Jones was what Philip Winter called a definite improvement. Nor had it taken much persuasion on Shaw's part to get her to agree to pose with him; she had been quite excited at the thought of posing with the famous Philip Winter who, without a doubt, was her favourite tennis player. Shaw didn't believe anything could go wrong now – but it did.

When he saw Kelly Jones, Philip Winter was all smiles and charm. He patted the bed beside him while the photographer readied his camera. 'Come up here then and sit next to me.' Smiling widely, Kelly perched herself on the bed next to him.

'Perhaps we could get Doctor Shaw into this one as well,' Hilary Templeton suggested.

Shaw looked at her in surprise. 'Me?' Then he thought, why not? 'Oh, all right. What do I have to do?'

'You could stand on the other side of Philip. Making some notes, or something. Looking concerned and professional, anyway.'

So the picture was taken, Philip Winter sitting up in the bed, his arm around Kelly Jones who was sitting next to him, while Raymond Shaw stood on the other side of the bed, looking concerned and professional as he pretended to jot something down in his notebook.

'Fine,' Winter said when the picture was taken. His arm was still around Kelly; their faces were very close together. 'Now let's have another one. Only without Doctor Shaw this time.'

Raymond Shaw smiled in satisfaction. He thought everything was going well.

More photographs were taken while Philip Winter held Kelly Jones close to him. Finally, Hilary Templeton said to the photographer, 'Thanks, Fred. I think that will do for the day.' She turned to the bed where Winter and Kelly were still smiling at each other. 'Thank you, Philip. We've got some very nice shots. And thank *you*, Nurse Jones. You've been a great help.'

Kelly climbed down off the bed and began to move across the room to the door. 'Wait a minute,'

Winter called after her. 'You're not going, are you?'

'I have to get back to my ward.'

'But I thought . . .' Puzzled, he looked up at Shaw. 'I thought Kelly here was going to be my nurse.'

'No.' Shaw shook his head. 'She only came to help out with the photographs. Nurse Warner has been assigned to you.'

Kelly Jones stood in the middle of the room, watching them. Winter was looking disappointed. 'I mean, Nurse Warner is a nice girl, and I've got nothing against her personally, but . . . well, I just get bad vibrations from her – you know?'

'No, I don't know,' Shaw said tersely.

'I mean, she's so . . . *gloomy*. Cold as a brass door knob. Couldn't she switch with Kelly here?'

'Well, I don't know . . .' Shaw turned to Kelly Jones into whose eyes a certain hardness had appeared.

'I don't think so, Mister Winter,' Kelly said quietly but firmly. 'I think *I'm* the one who's getting the bad vibrations now.' Winter's eyes widened in surprise. Shaw groaned inwardly; everything had been going so well until now. 'You might be a millionaire and the world's best tennis player,' she went on ruthlessly. 'But, as a human being, you leave a lot to be desired.' She looked across at Shaw. 'I think you should get Julie out of here, Doctor Shaw,' she said. 'She doesn't deserve the shabby treatment she's been getting from these people.'

With that, she swung on her heel and walked grandly out of the room.

'Well, I'll be damned,' Winter muttered peevishly after she had gone. 'The bloody cheek of the girl.' He looked extremely put out.

Embarrassed by what had happened, Shaw was profuse in his apologies. 'I really don't know what came over her,' he offered. 'I'll have a word with her, and see if we can't get this straightened out.' Winter was scarcely mollified. Taking a cigarette from the packet on the bedside table, he lit it with a solid gold lighter. 'I'm sure she didn't really mean it.'

Winter was smoking furiously. Hilary Templeton followed Shaw to the door. 'I trust we won't have any more such unpleasantness,' she said crisply.

'I can assure you it won't happen again, Miss Templeton,' Shaw said feelingly.

'I hope not, Doctor Shaw,' she said with real menace in her voice. 'For everyone's sake.'

'He's rude, he's arrogant and egotistical. He's inconsiderate of other people's feelings. The way he talked about Julie . . . He'll treat her like dirt, you mark my words.'

Brian Denham sighed. This was another problem, piled up on all the problems faced by the Medical Superintendent of a busy city hospital, that he just did not need. Something also that needed to be smoothed out in the best diplomatic manner. His job wasn't the easiest one in the world, that was for sure. 'I couldn't bear to be near the man,' Kelly said.

Denham looked at her, then at Julie Warner who was staring blankly back at him. He had to admit she wasn't exactly overladen with personality. He cleared his throat. 'We all have our share of difficult patients,' he said, 'but I'll agree that this one is somewhat exceptional.'

'Because he's rich?' Kelly asked drily.

It was below the belt, but Denham managed to weather the blow. The only way to approach this was to lay his cards fairly and squarely on the table. 'Well, in a way, yes.' He glanced at Raymond Shaw. 'That's why I asked you to come here. So we could discuss this.'

'I asked him to do it, actually,' Shaw explained to the two nurses.

Denham decided it was time to lob the ball into Shaw's court. 'This is *your* pet project in a way, Raymond. Why don't you tell them about it?'

Shaw leaned forward confidentially. 'This is between us, of course,' he said. 'You see, Philip Winter has almost – almost, mind – pledged two hundred thousand dollars towards our new Children's wing.'

Julie Warner showed some emotion at last. Her eyes widened behind her spectacles as she gave a soft gasp. Shaw nodded. The enormity of what was at stake had gotten through with no trouble at all. 'Miss Templeton has hinted that he may make the donation – and *I'm* hinting that two hundred thousand is a nice round figure.'

'It *is* a lot of money,' Julie Warner said, impressed.

'It certainly is,' Shaw confirmed. 'And we haven't got it yet.'

'I take it that means we have to give him whatever he wants.'

Which was putting it perhaps a little too baldly. Shaw gave Denham a quick, uncomfortable glance. 'Well . . . only within reason, I suppose.'

'But *only* within reason,' Denham supplied. He wanted to make that point absolutely clear.

Shaw was still leaning forward in his chair. His voice and manner were totally persuasive as he made an appeal to Kelly Jones. 'If it were any other patient in the world, I wouldn't ask this favour of you.'

'What favour is that?' Kelly asked with a lift of her eyebrows.

'To switch with Julie here. Take on Philip Winter's case. If you're willing, of course.'

'It's entirely your decision, Kelly,' Brian Denham said.

Kelly was hesitating. She looked doubtful. Shaw was still appealing to her. 'He's a vain, egotistical man. But he's also a very generous man – and we need his help.'

'Yes, Kelly,' Julie Warner urged. 'Go ahead and do it. I don't mind – really,' she said when Kelly looked at her in surprise.

'But . . . the principle.'

'If it's good for the hospital, then it's all right with me.'

'I still think it's wrong,' Kelly said stubbornly.

'Well, that's that then,' Shaw said to Denham with a resigned shrug.

Kelly was still turning the matter over in her mind. 'I have one condition,' she said at last.

'What's that?'

'That he apologises to Julie.'

Yes, Shaw thought gloomily, that was definitely that. He couldn't, for the life of him, see Philip Winter apologising to anyone.

But again he was wrong. Philip Warner thought it was a great idea, which, his manner seemed to imply, had originated solely from himself. No trouble at all, he assured Shaw who was taken aback by his unexpectedly co-operative attitude. And when he did apologise, it was with grace and charm. Shaw was impressed, and pleased; it seemed that now they had passed through that patch of rough water, it would be plain sailing from here on in. Philip Winter's donation, he thought, was already as good as being in the bag.

'What are you doing out of bed?'

'I'm three under par on the eighteenth green and two strokes ahead of . . .'

'Get back into bed this instant, Mister Winter,' Kelly snapped. 'There are some tests I want to run on you.'

She had found him putting golf balls into the metal waste container, his eyes narrowed against the smoke rising from the cigarette in the corner of his mouth. 'Yeah . . . well . . .' Winter lined up for another shot. Kelly eyed him distastefuly. A man who could bring his golf clubs into hospital with him had a damned hide. 'Just give me a couple of minutes.' He hit the ball. There was a clatter as it rolled into the waste container.

'Did you hear me, Mister Winter?'

'Yes, I did, Miss Jones.' He placed another ball on the floor in front of him. As he lined up for the next shot, Kelly crossed purposely to the waste bin and righted it. 'Hey, what are you doing?'

'The game's over, Mister Winter.' She pointed to the bed, 'Into bed.'

Winter glowered at her. 'I don't know who you think you are,' he growled, 'but I don't think I like your attitude.'

'You're not here to like my attitude,' Kelly told him grimly. 'You're here to do as you're told.'

Clearly angry now, he gestured towards the waste container. 'Put it back.'

'No.'

'Put it back,' he threatened, 'or I'll have you returned to the Public wards.'

Kelly moved briskly across to him. 'Go ahead,' she said tightly. 'You'd look a perfect fool after all the trouble you took to get me here in the first place. But you don't worry about looking a fool, do you? You always get your own way, don't you? Now . . .' she pointed imperiously to the bed again . . . 'you either get into bed this instant, or I'm leaving.'

He stared at here for a long moment, then with a shrug, clambered back into bed where Kelly took the cigarette from his mouth to make room for her thermometer.

'Doctor Rothwell is dropping by to have a look at you,' she said after she had taken his temperature.

'Terrific,' Winter said unenthusiastically, then, with more interest, asked her as she began to tidy the room, 'What are your plans for the future, Kelly?'

'I just want to be as good a nurse as possible.'

'Have you ever considered a career as a fashion model?'

'What?' She laughed. 'Oh, come on.'

'I mean it,' he said seriously. 'As it happens, I own part of a fashion magazine in the States. I've helped a lot of girls get started on the road to success.'

'I bet you have,' Kelly said drily.

'I'm serious.'

'I'm sure you are.'

It might have gone on like this for some time longer if Craig Rothwell hadn't entered the room just then. Kelly handed him Winter's chart. 'His temperature's stable at one hundred point five.'

'I see.' Craig examined the chart for a moment, then put it down. 'Let's have a listen then, shall we?' he said, fitting his stethoscope. Easing Winter forward, Kelly pulled up his pyjama top to leave his torso bare. Craig applied the stethoscope first to his back then his chest. 'Cough, please.' Winter obliged him with a cough. 'Again.' He straightened. Kelly gently pushed the patient back against the pillows. 'Do you smoke, Mister Winter?'

'A little.'

'A lot,' Kelly amended.

'I thought so.' Craig nodded. 'I'll just have a brief word with Doctor Shaw,' he told Kelly. He waved his hand to Winter as he headed for the door. 'See you later, Mister Winter. And I'd advise you go give up smoking.' He gestured to the golf club Winter had left propped up against the wall. 'Does wonders for your game.'

'There's no one more boring than a non-smoker,' Winter observed wrily, then coughed. He reached for his cigarettes.

Kelly held out her hand. 'Give.'

He hesitated, defiantly holding her look for a moment before handing her the packet with a great show of reluctance. 'Whose side are you on, anyway?'

'Yours.'

Philip Winter grimaced, then groaned as Carolyn Fielding bustled into the room, exclaiming, 'Oh, Philip, darling, there you are.'

It was visiting time. 'Oh God,' Winter muttered under his breath as his visitor bore down on him. 'Oh, Carolyn, look, I do have a lot of work . . .'

Kelly decided it was time to leave. 'I'll look in on you later, Mister Winter,' she said on her way to the door.

'Yes, all right.' As she let herself out of the room, she heard him saying behind her, 'Carolyn, I don't want to see you tonight. So will you please leave.'

'Craig will be assisting me on Philip's operation.'

'Then I'm sure he'll be in very good hands,' Hilary Templeton said, looking at Craig.

'Oh, yes,' Shaw assured her. 'It's a delicate operation, but a fairly straightforward one.'

'That's what I came to see you about,' Craig Rothwell told him.

'Oh?'

'I think we'll have to postpone it until the end of the week.'

'Postpone it? Why?'

'You can't do that,' Hilary Templeton protested.

Craig turned to her. 'Miss Templeton, what was Mister Winter doing before he came here? I mean, immediately before he came here.'

'He was in a yacht race. In Adelaide. He sponsored one of the boats.'

'That figures,' Craig said.

Shaw was frowning at the younger doctor. 'What are you driving at, Craig?'

'I'll have to run a sputum test, but I think he has a nasty case of pneumonia.'

'Damn!' Shaw exclaimed. Complications, complications all the way. Would nothing *ever* go smoothly? He had just assured Hilary Templeton that her employer would be up and about again by the twenty-fifth, in good time to open his new tennis camp just outside Los Angeles. Of course, he would have to use crutches for a while . . .

'That's ridiculous,' Hilary Templeton cried. 'It's just a smoker's cough.'

'I don't think so.'

'Doctor Shaw . . .' She was appealing to him.

'I'm sorry,' he said with an unhappy shake of his head. 'But if it *is* bronchitis, we couldn't possibly operate until it's cleared up.'

'Two or three days at least,' Craig informed her.

'My God,' Hilary Templeton said woefully. 'This is really going to upset his schedule.'

10

'I'm sorry, Miss Templeton, but I must ask you to leave. We have to get Mister Winter ready now for his operation.'

Hilary Templeton looked helplessly at Philip Winter who had just finished snapping a set of instructions to someone on his specially installed telephone. She raised the sheaf of papers she was holding. 'These are still waiting for your signature.'

'Nurse's orders, Hilary,' he said with a brief glance at Kelly Jones. 'They'll wait.'

Craig Rothwell pressed his stethoscope to Winter's chest. 'Sounds good,' he said after listening for a few moments. 'I think you'll do just fine.'

'Where's Doctor Shaw?' Winter demanded.

'He'll be waiting in the theatre when they wheel you in,' Kelly told him.

Straightening, Craig Rothwell removed the stethoscope from his ears. 'I'll let Doctor Shaw know you're ready for surgery.' He nodded to Hilary Templeton, then to Winter. 'Good luck, Mister Winter.'

'At Shaw's prices, I hope I don't need it,' Winter said caustically.

Hilary Templeton replaced the papers in her briefcase and stood up. 'Good luck, Philip.'

'Thank you, Hilary.'

Kelly was preparing Winter's needle. When they were alone, Winter smiled up at her. 'Will you be there to nurse me back from oblivion, Nurse Jones?' he asked.

'That's what I'm paid to do, Mister Winter.'

Suddenly, he reached up, and grabbing her arm, pulled her down to him. He kissed her fully on the lips. 'In case I don't pull through the operation,' he said with a smirk as he released her.

She slapped his face. 'And that's just in case you do,' she said coldly.

Doctor Shaw was very pleased with the way the operation had gone. There had been no complications whatsoever. After Winter had been taken back to his room, he allowed Hilary Templeton a brief visit, 'just to make sure the great man is still alive'.

He was alive, but he wasn't exactly kicking at the moment; he was still unconscious. Hilary Templeton and Kelly Jones stood on either side of the bed, looking down at him. 'Money is honey, my little sonny,' Hilary Templeton murmured. 'And a rich man's joke is always funny.' She looked up at Kelly. 'Sometimes I feel almost sorry for him.'

'How long have you worked for him?' Kelly asked.

'Six years,' Hilary replied. 'Six fantastic years.' She sighed. 'I don't know . . . I suppose many women would envy me, being private secretary to a man like Philip Winter. Yes, it does have its moments.' She gazed down at her unconscious employer whose face, Kelly decided, was rather sweet in repose. 'He'd never marry, you know. He'll give a girl anything . . . almost anything she could wish for . . . except a wedding ring.'

Kelly was stung by this statement. As if she had any intention . . . 'I assure you,' she said acidly, 'the thought never crossed my mind.'

Hilary Templeton smiled faintly. 'I've seen the way he looks at you. I know that look. I know it very well. God, how many times have I seen it? Just be careful – that's all the advice I can give you. Don't expect more than he's prepared to give. You'll only get hurt if you do.'

'It's over, Carolyn. There's no use trying to see him any more.'

'I don't know what you mean.'

Hilary opened her bag, and extracting the cheque, placed it on the table between them. 'It's a cheque for ten thousand dollars,' she explained. 'Philip asked me to give it to you. It's his way of saying goodbye.'

Carolyn Fielding stared at her dumbly. Hilary expected a scene. Sometimes there were scenes; sometimes there weren't, when the girl, perhaps having already seen the writing on the wall, would take the money and be thankful. 'You knew it wouldn't last. They never do, Philip would prefer it if you didn't try to see him again.'

'I want to talk to him,' Carolyn said softly.

Oh dear, Hilary thought, she was going to be difficult after all. 'You'll be wasting your time. Just how many cheques like this one do you think I've written? Would you like me to tell you?'

Carolyn Fielding sat there like a woman whose world had suddenly come crushing down around her head. Hilary knew that look; she had seen it often enough before.

'I know you're busy, as I am, so I'll come straight to the point. The operation seems to have been performed satisfactorily. I'm impressed with the efficiency of the organisation, and of the staff . . .' Winter glanced up at Kelly . . . 'particularly the nursing staff. However, I do have to say that your Doctor Shaw is becoming something of a nuisance.'

Winter had been dictating a letter to Hilary Templeton when Brian Denham had come to the room in response to his summons. 'Oh?' Denham raised his eyebrows; this was the last thing he had expected to hear.

'He is, of course, an excellent surgeon,' Winter went on. 'But his constant angling for money is something less than subtle, and frankly, it's beginning to bore me.'

Denham regarded him steadily. The man was playing games, of course; he was juggling with them. 'If you're referring to the Children's wing,' he said stiffly, 'it was my understanding that you promised him a donation some time ago.'

'Well . . .' Winter shrugged . . . 'I might have said I would consider it.' He sighed. 'Oh, all right, if it will get the man off my back, he can have his donation. Miss Templeton can draw up a cheque.'

Hilary Templeton made a note on her pad. 'For what amount?' she asked.

'Oh . . .' Winter considered for a moment. 'Give him a thousand. That should keep him happy.'

'Are you ready for a visitor?'

'Who?'

'Your friend,' Kelly said. 'Carolyn Fielding. She's waiting in the foyer.'

The smile with which Winter had greeted Kelly abruptly vanished. He looked stonily at Hilary Templeton. 'I thought you gave her her marching orders.'

'I did,' Hilary said impassively. 'On Friday night.'

'And the cheque?'

'Ten thousand dollars. As usual.'

Winter looked back up at Kelly. 'Tell her she's been paid off. I don't want to see her.'

Kelly had never heard anything quite so brutal. 'And *I* don't get paid to say things like that to other human beings,' she snapped.

'Then just tell her I'm busy,' Winter said after a brief pause.

Winter was just getting the hang of the crutches that had been supplied to him. Now, supporting himself on one of them, he was standing beside his bed, opening letters with an antique Italian dagger while Hilary Templeton sat on the other side of the bed with pad and pencil at the ready. As Carolyn Fielding came into the room, he glared at her. 'What are you doing here, Carolyn?' he demanded.

She was carrying a bunch of flowers. 'I came to see you,' she said brightly. She held the flowers out to him. 'Peace offering.' When Winter said nothing, her brightness faded. 'Philip, I know you didn't mean it. It *was* a joke, wasn't it?'

'No joke, Carolyn,' he said flatly. 'There's a natural end to everything, to every relationship. And ours has reached that natural end.'

Carolyn's face was crumbling. Her eyes filled with tears. 'Just a year . . . six months . . . I wasn't ready. I . . . if I *was* ready, it would be all right.' Putting down her pad and pencil, Hilary Templeton rose from her chair and left the room. Carolyn Fielding was still staring at Philip Winter with an imploring expression. 'Please, Philip . . .'

Winter placed the Italian dagger he had been using as a letter opener on the table beside him. He shook his head. 'No, Carolyn.'

'Please . . .' She took a hesitant step closer to him. The tears were coursing down her cheeks. 'Since Friday night I've been trying to think what I've been doing wrong . . . if there's some way I've been irritating you. I . . .'

'Yes, there is,' Winter said evenly. 'You're trying to hang on when it's finished. If you really do wish to please me, you'll walk out of that door, right now.'

She stared at him. She was breaking up, disintegrating. With a sob, she moved closer to him. As if automatically, her hand closed over the handle of the Italian dagger Winter had placed on the table only seconds before. Then, quickly, before Winter realised what she was doing, she brought up the dagger and plunged it into his abdomen.

Backing away from her, Winter stared in mounting horror at the handle of the dagger that was protuding from his abdomen, surrounded by a spreading patch of blood. He staggered, then slowly, as Carolyn ran towards the door, slumped down beside the bed. At the door, Carolyn collided with Hilary Templeton who was just coming back into the room. Seeing Winter beside the bed, Hilary hurried towards him. 'Little bitch,' Winter muttered as she dropped to her knees beside him. 'She . . . she . . . stabbed me.'

Kelly Jones was just coming into the room. When she saw Hilary kneeling beside the inert form of Philip Winter, reaching for the handle of the dagger that was embedded in his abdomen, she rushed across to her side. She grabbed Hilary's wrist. 'Don't move it,' she cried urgently. 'You could kill him.'

Shaw sat with Brian Denham in his office studying the plans that had been drawn up for the new Children's wing when Helen Gordon hurried in to tell him that he was wanted at the operating theatre immediately. It was an emergency. Philip Winter had a knife wound in the abdomen.

Denham stared at her in amazement. This was just what he needed. 'He's been *stabbed*?'

'All Doctor Rothwell said was that he had a knife wound in the abdomen.'

'Well, I'm not going to say he had it coming,' Shaw remarked as he moved to the door. 'So I'm not going to say it.'

'Did Craig say how bad it is?' Denham asked Helen.

'He said they won't know until they've operated. But he's still alive.'

Small consolation that was. 'If he's going to get himself stabbed,' Denham complained, 'why does it have to happen in *my* hospital?'

'This is the last place I would have expected to find you,' Hilary Templeton said. She had thought Carolyn Fielding would have been miles away from the hospital. But it appeared that she hadn't even left the hospital. Hilary had been astonished to find her sitting morosely in the visitors' area downstairs.

'How is he?' Carolyn asked dully.

'Still alive.'

'I love him, Hilary.'

'Do you want to prove that?'

'He's going to be all right, isn't he?' She was looking hopefully up at Hilary.

'I hope so.' Carolyn began to cry. 'Stop that,' Hilary said sharply. Carolyn stopped crying. 'You realise, of course, what the media will make of this.' Carolyn nodded. 'Now, at this moment in time, you have no choice,' Hilary went on relentlessly. 'You can walk out of here in five minutes, and once you've gotten over your broken heart, end up leading a reasonable sort of life. Or you can spend the next few years in gaol and be known far and wide for the rest of your life as the lady who stabbed Philip Winter because he dumped her.' Carolyn nodded slowly. 'That's the choice then. Walk out of here and forget it happened. Or ruin your life.' Carolyn nodded again. 'So what will you do?'

'Walk.'

'Good. Now do you want some advice?' When Carolyn made no response to this, she gave it, anyway. 'Anyone who can't pocket a ten thousand dollar cheque and walk away from a Philip Winter is just not cut out for this sort of life. You're on the wrong circuit. Marry a nice man, live in a nice suburb, give him nice children.'

'That was what I was going to do,' Carolyn said quietly. 'I *was* engaged to a nice man – remember? When I met Philip.'

Hilary smiled down at her. 'Snap.'

Carolyn stared bleakly up at her. 'Why don't you take your own advice?'

It was an awkward question. 'I've . . . I guess I've become used to it.'

'You love him, don't you?'

'I've grown to be like him,' Hilary Templeton replied tautly.

'Luckiest man alive,' Shaw pronounced. 'The blade missed the liver, spleen and lung, glanced past the aorta by . . .' his thumb and forefinger were almost touching . . . 'that much. Didn't catch stomach or intestine.'

The operation was almost over. It was just a matter of closing him up again. Brian Denham peered down at the patient. 'So no intestinal matter has been allowed into the peritoneal cavity . . .

'Nope.' Shaw was stitching deftly. 'Lucky boy.' He looked up at Craig Rothwell on the other side of the table. 'Okay, Doctor Rothwell, finish the closing.'

Denham moved away from the table with him. 'What happened?'

'Someone got angry with him.'

'No chance it was an accident then?'

Shaw chuckled softly and shook his head. 'Name your odds.'

'He couldn't have done it himself?' Denham asked hopefully.

'Hardly the suicidal type,' Shaw opined.

'He was on crutches. He could have been opening a letter, slipped . . .'

'The hell he did, Brian,' Shaw said impatiently. 'He was stabbed, and you know it.'

Brian Denham's main concern was the unfavourable publicity the incident would attract to the hospital. Helen Gordon wondered why he should be so worried. Philip Winter had told Doctor Rothwell it was an accident. Winter's secretary had said the same thing. Where was the problem?

'Abdominal wounds like that are tricky,' Denham told her. 'Suppose we *do* lose him. There'll be a coroner's hearing. Doctor Shaw is of the opinion that he was stabbed by someone. If I'm asked why I didn't report it to the police.'

'Perhaps you *should* report it,' Helen suggested.

'I'm thinking about it,' Denham told her seriously. 'Winter would deny it, of course.'

There was a knock on the door of his office. Helen Gordon was crossing the floor to open it when it did open and Hilary Templeton appeared. 'There was no one in the outer office,' she said apologetically.

'Come in, Miss Templeton,' Denham invited from behind his desk. 'How can I help you?'

As Helen Gordon returned to her own office, Hilary Templeton advanced into the room and sat down on the chair Denham was indicating to her. 'I want you to talk to your staff,' she said. 'I want them to be very clear that what happened to Mister Winter today was an accident.'

'You're sure of that, are you?'

'Perfectly sure,' she replied calmly. 'I was there when it happened. He was reaching for some papers. One of his crutches slipped, and he fell onto the floor.'

Right onto the blade of a knife which just happened to be there. Denham looked at her dubiously.

She was staring back at him defiantly. 'I was

there.'

'Were you really?'

'I think I can speak for Mister Winter when I say that he *won't* be suing the hospital and Doctor Shaw for negligence.'

'He wouldn't collect, Miss Templeton,' Denham said quietly.

'The law suit wouldn't do *your* career any good, Doctor,' Hilary said sweetly. As I say, he *won't* sue – as long as no silly stories get around.'

'Silly stories to the effect that . . .'

'That he was stabbed,' Hilary finished for him. 'I hope I'm making myself clear.'

'Yes, you are, Miss Templeton,' Denham said in clipped tones. 'I quite understand that you're threatening me. I also understand that you cannot be speaking for Mister Winter who has been unconscious since this incident happened.' He stood up. 'I intend to speak to him when he regains consciousness.'

'I'm sure he'll call for you.' Hilary Templeton was also on her feet.

'In my hospital,' Denham curtly informed her, 'he'll speak to me whether he calls or not.'

'I understand there's been some speculation about how I was injured,' Philip Winter said. 'I am now going to tell you what really happened so that speculation can be put to rest.' He spoke as if he were chairing a board meeting. Shaw and Denham had just arrived. Hilary Templeton was sitting beside Winter's bed. Kelly Jones was on the other side of the bed. 'I was reaching for some papers,' Winter continued, 'when I slipped and fell on my paper knife. Miss Templeton was a witness to that.' He was looking directly at Brian Denham. 'I won't take kindly to any suggestion that I was deliberately stabbed.'

Brian Denham brought up what he had just learned from Kelly Jones, which, on the face of it, placed an entirely different complexion on the matter. 'Nurse Jones here tells me that when she came in she heard you saying, "Little bitch stabbed me".'

Winter glared fiercely at Kelly. 'She misheard me,' he told Denham. 'What I said, in fact, was, "Bitch of a thing . . . stabbed myself".'

'What on earth did that mean?' Denham asked.

'I was cursing the knife.'

Denham looked at Kelly. 'Do you think you *could* have misheard, Miss Jones?'

Winter was glaring at her again. Kelly looked uncertain. 'Perhaps I did,' she said at last.

'Fine.' Winter smiled broadly. 'Now we can all forget the whole incident.' He nodded to Denham and Shaw. 'Thank you, gentlemen,' he said then turned to Hilary Templeton. 'Now you'll have put back Europe a week.' Philip Winter was making a rapid recovery from his operation.

It wasn't too difficult to work out how the fire had started in Philip Winter's room. He had been smoking again. He had been careless. He had almost died.

The room was still reeking with smoke. Winter had managed to press the buzzer before collapsing, overcome with smoke inhalation. The fire was in the waste bin. It had been quickly extinguished. Craig Rothwell was holding the oxygen mask to Winter's face. 'Just how did a fire start in this room, Doctor Rothwell,' Hilary Templeton demanded to know.

Winter had regained consciousness. Craig Rothwell took the oxygen mask from his face. 'In the waste bin,' he replied coldly. 'And don't snap at me, Miss Templeton. I don't like it.'

Raymond Shaw had been having dinner across the road at Bunny's Place when he had been urgently summoned back to the hospital. He also wanted to know how the fire had started. Craig Rothwell had told him that when it started Winter had tried to put it out, but had collapsed before he managed to do so.

'I would like to know how a fire started in the waste bin,' Hilary Templeton persisted. 'I would also like to know where Nurse Jones was at the time. She *is* supposed to be Mister Winter's private nurse after all.' She gave Kelly a withering look.

'I had just left the room to speak with Doctor Denham,' Kelly said.

'Nurse Jones has constantly asked Mister Winter not to smoke,' Craig said. 'And just as constantly he has ignored her orders.'

Winter smiled weakly up at Shaw who had just been examining him with his stethoscope. 'Guilty, Doctor Shaw.'

'It's very difficult, Doctor Shaw,' Kelly said crossly, 'when the patient blatantly ignores your instructions.'

Shaw had had enough. He was very angry. He glowered down at his patient. 'I've taken about as much from you as any reasonable man can,' he said savagely. 'Now I'm laying it on the line – and to hell with your damned donation. You are a *patient* in this hospital, and as long as you are, you will obey my instructions to the letter.' He swung to face Kelly. 'Nurse, if this man gives you any more trouble you are to report it straight to me.' He turned to Winter again. 'You're damned lucky the wound didn't burst open.' He studied his patient grimly. 'If you *do* wish to transfer to another hospital we'll be happy to oblige you. You can let either Doctor Denham or myself know what you've decided in the morning.'

'He's got an impressive temper our Doctor Shaw, hasn't he?'

'Justified I'd say, however,' Kelly said. She had brought a fresh jug of water into the room. She should have been off duty already, but the night nurse was late.

'You would say that, would you?'

'I would also say that I think you're a pain in the neck.'

Winter gave her a slow smile. 'You have style, Nurse Jones,' he said admiringly.

'Is there anything else you need before I go? And we can do without the "goodnight kiss" routine.

That has worn just a little thin.'

'Whatever you say,' Winter said with a shrug. 'Would you sit and talk to me for a minute?'

Kelly thought about it. 'All right then,' she said, sitting down beside the bed. 'Just for a minute.'

'Why do they call you Kelly?' Winter asked.

'My Dad wanted a boy. Kelly was a compromise. Sometimes I regret the fact that I wasn't born a boy. I might have turned out to be like you. Very rich, I mean.'

'Do you envy me my wealth?'

'Not really,' Kelly replied. 'I've always liked to be liked for myself.' Winter winced slightly as the blow struck home. Kelly delivered another blow. 'I thought the way you treated that poor Fielding girl was the cruellest thing I've seen.'

'But you don't understand.' Philip Winter was on the defensive.

'Perhaps I don't,' Kelly conceded. 'But if that's what money does to people, then I'm glad I'm poor.'

'I wonder,' Winter drawled reflectively. 'I guess I owe you my life,' he said after a brief pause.

'Should I play "Hearts and Flowers"?' Kelly asked drily.

'It's true nevertheless,' Winter said with sincerity. 'I'm in your debt, and I'm a man who has always paid his debts. Rich men can be quite ethical that way – surprisingly. Now, Kelly, I would like to do something for you – to repay you for saving my life.'

Kelly was becoming embarrassed. She shifted

uneasily on her chair. 'Don't worry about it, please. It's my job.'

Winter was watching her intently. 'How does a world trip appeal to you? Would you like to see the world?'

'I've already seen the world,' Kelly replied. 'Or enough of it. And I can't say I was too impressed by what I've seen. That's why I came home.' She rose to her feet. 'I'm afraid you'll have to get yourself another girl, Mister Winter. But . . .' she smiled down at him . . . 'if you've nothing to do with the money, you might keep in mind the new Children's wing. They could do with it.' She began to move across the room to the door. 'Now, if you need anything – and I do mean urgently – just press the buzzer. Goodnight. Sleept tight.'

'I'm a man who's used to getting what he wants, Kelly,' Winter said. 'No matter how long it takes.'

In one of the side rooms set aside for visitors a still angry Raymond Shaw was laying down the law to Hilary Templeton, while Craig Rothwell leaned against the wall with an air of detachment.

'Either he does as he's told, or I want him out of here. Let someone else put up with his demands and his irresponsible attitude. 'He raised his eyes towards the ceiling. 'God protect us all from multi-millionaires,' he intoned. He pointed a finger at Hilary who was sitting on a bench nursing a card-board container of coffee. 'He's a pain – that's what he is.'

'I think you're being quite unreasonable, Doctor

Shaw,' Hilary said with a frown.

'Oh, *do* you?' Shaw retorted. 'The fact that he almost set the hospital on fire, that he ignores anyone who tries to tell him anything, his constant rudeness to the staff, and the fact that he seems to regard his hospitalisation as a convenient publicity stunt . . . well, let me tell you, Miss Templeton, how you've managed to put up with that guy for so long simply amazes me.'

'I admit he's difficult,' Hilary Templeton said quietly. 'For most of his life, he's been used to having his own way. He's also an extremely heavy smoker. Do you expect him to stop just like that? For some, it might be easy. For Philip Winter it's not.'

'I'm inclined to agree, sir,' Craig Rothwell said. 'I think it's been rough on him. He's not a man who's used to being cooped up. Nor is he used to taking orders.'

Perhaps he did have a point, Shaw conceded. 'Let me ask you this, Miss Templeton,' he said more reasonably. 'What would have happened if Nurse Jones hadn't been on hand at that very moment? Would you have accepted the responsibility – the blame – if Winter had suffocated?'

'I know what you're saying,' Hilary murmured.

'It would have been laid at the door of this hospital,' Shaw asserted. 'It would have been our fault.'

'Yes, I know.' Hilary was frowning down at her coffee.

'God knows we've already one near miss with

that woman stabbing him.' He was making a stab of his own.

'It was an accident,' Hilary said firmly.

Shaw gave her a sceptical look. 'Imagine if *that* had got into the papers.'

'It didn't,' Hilary said. 'And it won't. I'll talk to him. First thing in the morning.' She stood up. 'I'll let you know then what he has decided.'

'Well, have you given it any thought?'

'About what?'

'My proposition.'

'Yes, I have thought about it, Kelly said. 'I've decided not to accept.'

'Good Lord, why not?' Philip Winter gave a sigh of exasperation. 'I'm offering you a world trip, in luxury, the most exciting cities in Europe and Asia. How can you pass *that* up?'

'Very easily,' Kelly replied. 'Anyway, that's my prerogative.'

Philip Winter was shaking his head in bemusement. 'I don't understand you, Kelly. Most women would jump at the chance. So what is it you want?'

'Well . . .'

'Then there *is* something you want,' Winter said quickly.

'Maybe . . .'

Winter was beginning to show impatience. 'Let's hear it then.'

'I want it made quite clear that none of this has anything to do with the donation you're making to the hospital.' He had already told Doctor Shaw that he wanted a photographer on hand when he passed over the cheque.

'Done,' Winter said with a smile. 'I'm a man of my word.'

'Fine.' Kelly smiled back at him. 'Now I'm not against the idea of accompanying you on a world trip as your private nurse. but I just want it to be worthwhile.'

Winter sighed. 'All right, how much?'

'I think my services would be worth easily forty thousand dollars.'

Winter gave a soft whistle. 'Forty thousand . . .'

'In advance.'

'Blimey . . .'

'Our contract would last six months from the date of my resignation here. No longer.' Winter watched her in an awed silence as she continued. 'And if you have any notions about getting me into the cot, you can forget it. That privilege is reserved for the man who places a little gold band on my finger.'

'You're joking, aren't you?' Winter groaned.

'No, Mister Winter. And I'm worth it. If only from the publicity angle.'

Craig Rothwell breezed into the room. 'How's it going?'

'Just lovely,' Winter gritted through clenched teeth. 'Just bloody lovely.'

'All right, Philip, out with it. What's troubling you?'

'Nothing's troubling me.'

Philip Winter was lying back in his bed, holding a tennis ball in each hand, squeezing them with his fingers to strengthen his hand muscles. 'I've known you for a long time,' Hilary Templeton said patiently, 'and I can tell when you're nervous and irritable.'

'It's nothing a good work out on the court wouldn't cure,' Winter remarked sourly.

'Turned you down, has she?'

Winter was staring up at the ceiling. 'What *are* you talking about?'

'Kelly Jones. You know very well what I mean.'

'Mercenary little . . . She's reaching for the moon if she thinks she can dictate to *me*.'

'I'd say she has a pretty sound business mind,' Hilary observed. Winter looked at her disapprovingly, but said nothing. 'You're not used to dancing someone else's tune, are you?'

'I'll get her,' he muttered.

'Perhaps. But this one won't come cheap. Not like Carolyn.'

'But I'll still get her.'

'Have you ever *not* had anything you wanted, Philip?' she asked him.

Winter squeezed his tennis balls and gave her a long, hard look. 'Depends on how badly I want it,' he said at last.

The looked up as the subject of their speculations entered the room and greeted them. 'Time for your temperature check, Mister Winter,' Kelly told him.

They were both staring at her as she placed the thermometer in Winter's mouth. Then, removing the tennis ball from his left hand, took his pulse. Winter removed the thermometer with his free hand and turned his head to Hilary Templeton. 'Hilary, would you draw up an agreement between Nurse Jones and myself,' he instructed. 'It should stipulate that all her demands will be met regarding her employment as my private nurse for a six-month period. Give her whatever she wants,' he said as Kelly stared at him in amazement.